THE ACCLAIM FO
JUDITH McCONNELL STEELE s
ANGEL OF ESPERANÇA

✦ ✦ ✦

"Judith McConnell Steele's *The Angel of Esperança* casts a spell like a gossamer net. Every word, every character, every double-door detail offers magic, emotion and meaning. This reader was too gladly captured."

– Clay Morgan, author of *Santiago and the Drinking Party* and *The Boy Who Spoke Dog*, Boise State University writing professor and director of The Story Initiative

"Judith Steele writes prose like a visionary angel, prose that delights with imagery and hypnotizes with seamless narration, flowing as naturally as the river beside her little town of Esperança. Reminiscent of Gabriel Garcia Marquez, Steele reinvents the mythic tale of star-crossed lovers in a sleepy town beset by mysterious events that bemuse and dislocate with tragic consequences. Mesmerizing in its scope and originality, the story reminds us what draws us to read novels and experience wonder at the ways of the world. You'll fall in love with this dark prince and the fair young princess he woos and marries, a young woman warned by her mother to never cut her hair for it will wind itself around her husband's heart and hold him close to her forever..."

– Jonis Agee, author of 13 books including *Strange Angels* and *The River Wife*, professor of creative writing and 20th-century fiction at the University of Nebraska

"This new telling of La Llorona begins 'Late at night, in the faraway town' and doesn't let you go until it's finished with you. Fantastic!"

"From the haunting opening to the searing conclusion *The Angel of Esperança* explores the ecology of emotion. This elegantly expressed story of romantic, filial, maternal and familial love virtually shimmers on the page. It exists in a nameless country in an undefined recent past. The plot is a fable of love, loss and redemption. Judith McConnell Steele's novel can be read in a sitting. The narrative is executed with a precise and sure hand, the writing is elegant, the characters complex and the setting casts a magical glow. This is grand fiction writing—immersive and rewarding."

THE
ANGEL OF
ESPERANÇA

✦ Judith McConnell Steele ✦

Judith McConnell Steele

Mill Park Publishing
Eagle, Idaho

Mill Park Publishing
www.MillParkPublishing.com

Mill Park Publishing
www.MillParkPublishing.com

Text copyright ©2013 by Judith McConnell Steele
Cover artwork: "Night," Edward Robert Hughes (1851-1914), watercolor and bodycolour on paper. Private collection. Permission by Bridgeman Art Library, New York.
Book cover and design by Sarah Tregay
Author photo by Diane Ronayne

ISBN: 978-0-9883980-5-4
Printed in USA

Mill Park Publishing
Eagle, ID 83616

www.MillParkPublishing.com

To Dick, who gives me love, encouragement
and a healthy dose of laughter every day.

To my beloved parents, June and Taylor McConnell,
who held me close yet let me fly at every step of my journey.

And to the good people of Brazil,
who took me in when I was unaware
and taught me how to live.

Chapter 1

✦ ✦ ✦

LATE AT NIGHT, in the faraway town of Esperança, a light burns in a lonely tower. A warm wind drifting through the town carries the mournful notes of the woman in the tower. Her voice rises into the wind, rippling the fronds of the coconut trees lining the town square, then drops low, insistent.

The people know who is shut in the tower. They never mention a name, afraid that to talk about the moans would make them louder. The sound invades their sleep. Men take their hammocks inside and hang them on hooks sunk deep in mud and wattle walls, close wooden shutters even when the air is stifling. Women stuff their ears with bits ripped from their handkerchiefs, welcome their babies' cries in the night to drown out the dreadful laments.

On nights when there is no light in the tower, the towns-people awake refreshed and nervous—"Has she run away? Is she dead?" The next night, the crying starts up, reassuring the town that all is as before. They will not sleep; their master will have no rest. He will come to his factory with

1

his hair wild and his suit rumpled. He will stare at them with burning eyes and work them half to death or not at all. All will be exactly as it has been for the last five weeks.

◆ ◆ ◆

Before Helena was shut in the tower, Esperança lived up to its name, "Hope."

It is not a beautiful town, flung onto the vast plain like a tattered map lying in the gutter. Still, it has its own squat church, hunkered on one side of the square, and Dona Ana's mercantile and bar slung along the other side like the devil's choice. A few of the mud houses lining the flat streets are spread with a prosperous layer of white plaster. Red tile roofs have replaced some of the palm thatch.

Women waiting for their morning coffee to boil on kerosene burners can buy fresh sugar buns from a neighbor's backyard oven. Men walking home from a hot day in the cement factory south of town can pay two centavos for a banana popsicle from a refrigerator set on a friend's front porch.

Dirt streets start out purposefully from the dusty square but soon meander off into the dry land that stretches from the ocean east of Esperança to the western jungle that looms green and hungry in people's dreams. The main street gives out north of town at the banks of the sadly misnamed Rio Branco which flows muddy brown most of the year. In the great rains, when water pours from God's grey metal pitcher, the river churns up out of its banks, traditionally taking along several mud houses with it. Always the same houses.

The occupants accept their fate, rebuild in a day. They are fishermen, marked by the gouged rings of flesh torn from their legs and hands by the piranhas living in the Rio Branco. The fishermen wade out every day except Sunday, praying to all their gods to send them anything but piranhas in their nets.

They are the only men not working in Sr. Machado's cement factory. They sell their catfish and soapfish to the maids in his large house, to Dona Ana, to housewives looking for something fresh for the midday meal.

Occasionally, they sell their catch to the captains of the two large canoes chugging down river every Friday with their precious cargo of girls dressed in the tidy blue and white uniforms of the Escola de Nossa Senhora.

Every Monday morning, the same canoes, painted with scenes from the Blessed Mother's life, pass Esperança on their way from the capital city to Nossa Senhora. The girls, shaded by striped canvas awnings, sit facing each other on long benches built into the boats' curving hulls. They drink cafezinhos laced with creamy milk and brown chunk sugar, eat the glazed buns served on a silver tray by two cabin boys in white waiter jackets. They gaze dreamily at Esperança and think about the prince who rode away with their Helena.

The canoes sway through the water, urged on by their pulsing engines. The girls ride without concern out of their mothers' arms and pretty villas in the dirty capital city to the pristine rooms and courtyards of the school where they learn penmanship, needlework, piano and voice, how to set a tea table and how to mount a horse.

It was from the river bank that Sr. Machado first glimpsed the lovely Helena. He was riding his horse, Ouro Preto, near the water's edge on a placid afternoon when the first canoe from the Escola de Nossa Senhora rounded an upstream bend in the river and floated past him. She was seated on the bench nearest him, facing away. All he saw was a glossy brown braid lying against a slender neck.

The next Monday, he was up before dawn, driving his cook frantic with orders for the whitest shirt and the hottest cafezinho. He arrived early at the bank of the Rio Branco. Ouro Preto, sensing his master's nerves, paced and pranced until the canoe's engine sounded its arrival.

She sat in exactly the same spot on the same bench. Just as she glided by him, she turned to speak to a classmate seated next to her, and he saw her graceful profile. He stayed on the bank, still mounted on the now quiet Ouro, long after the canoe was gone, long after the sun was high, contemplating that profile. He knew he must have her. He knew, for the first time since he was a child, that something he wanted might be denied him.

The next Friday, when the canoe rounded the bend, he thought for one moment that she wasn't on board. Then he realized that she had chosen a seat on the opposite side, that she was, as the boat slid by in a long glissando, looking at him. The answer in her blue eyes was "Yes" and "Yes."

Chapter 2

+ + +

Rain, a good omen in the parched land of Esperança, fell heavily the evening Helena and Sr. Machado were married.

Helena's mother had always envisioned her only daughter's wedding in the cathedral where she and Helena's father were married by the archbishop. That day the sun was bright; the cathedral's lacy spires pierced the clear sky as if sending word of the marriage straight to heaven. The blessed Virgin Mary, her calm face lit by the blaze of candles surrounding her blue robes and small feet, smiled down on them from her niche to the right of the high altar. Seven attendants, in a blue to match the Virgin's flowing gown, stood with Isabel to catch her if she swooned. Seven young men, including the bride and groom's five brothers, stood up bravely beside Julio, the youngest of them all.

The archbishop, resplendent in gold and white, outshone the bride. It was only right, Isabel always said to herself. The church and all her glory should burn brighter than any bride, especially a humble girl who had almost wed herself to Christ instead of the stranger who stood beside her in his solemn black suit.

A stranger he was then and a stranger he remained. What they had between them, in place of ease or under-standing, was their children. Two strong sons came first, then a tiny daughter who lived only hours, fading quickly to make room for Helena, born nine months and twelve days after her sweet sister's death.

As soon as Helena emerged, Isabel became fearful. This beautiful child seemed bewitched, staring at her mother when she was laid at her breast, not suckling, not crying, just looking at her with what seemed to Isabel a mixture of curiosity and judgment.

At that very moment, gazing into her daughter's navy eyes, Isabel decided Helena must learn early the ways of womanhood and the church. She must be disciplined care-fully, a task her mother imagined would be difficult. She must be married off not only well but quickly, to protect her from the hunger Isabel saw lying in the depths of her daughter's already steady eyes. She must be saved from her passion by a safe coupling with a stable man.

When Helena was barely two, her mother began pre-paring her for her future life, teaching her to care for her-self—wash her face, brush her teeth not once but twice every noon, fold her clothes into a neat bundle for the laundress, say her nightly prayers to Mother Mary and her own mother's favorite saints. Only her hair remained in her mother's care.

"Never cut it," her mother would remind her as she trimmed the dark, curling ends. "Never be boastful or proud. Let it be your secret glory. It will be beautiful after your looks are gone."

And later, "Braid it always. One braid will show the world you are a chaste woman. Keep it long for your husband. It will wrap itself around his heart and keep him fast to you."

Even with the training she had given her child, Sr. Machado's request for Helena's hand upset Isabel. She was shocked that her daughter, only 17 and still in school uniform, would be seen as a wife. Isabel knew nothing of the man or his family. She recognized the Machado name, had heard of the sugar cane plantation somewhere beyond the terrifying borders of her city and her dreams. The family name was stamped on the heavy brown paper bags of sugar delivered to her kitchen door every two weeks. It was scrawled in lush script on the labels of the rum bottles Julio kept in a glass cabinet by his leather reading chair in the library. It was, she realized after reading Sr. Machado's first brief, somewhat curt note to her husband, on other cans and boxes in her kitchen cupboards.

So the man had money, the basic but barest requirement for a suitor. From friends who had friends on neighboring plantations, she learned that Sr. Machado had cut himself off from the family home, walled himself up in his factory in a small town with a church visited only occasionally by a true priest and a young one at that. It seemed the devil had taken hold of her daughter.

This information she passed along to Julio, assuming, despite long years of living with him, that he would agree with her. Instead, he came home from dinner in the city with Sr. Machado and said only, "He is a good man. He will provide well."

Still, she heard Julio questioning his daughter the next evening behind the closed door of his study.

"Why this man? I will give you anyone, anything you wish."

"I want him, Father."

He had appeared on the river bank, a handsome man on horseback, looking so intensely at her that she felt his eyes on her before she turned slightly to glance back at the receding figure. His image stayed with her, as though she had stared too long at the sun. She could not free herself of him. She did not want to.

He was nothing like the men she knew in the city, the boys she met in carefully chaperoned dances under the watchful eyes of her mother. He was comfortable in a country that Helena saw as wild, unguarded. With him by her side, she could leave her schoolgirl life and ride into a land so endless it looked like freedom.

◆ ◆ ◆

In a message her mother allowed her to read, Sr. Machado was invited to Helena's house for a meal. He accepted immediately. Helena did not know if trips to the city were a sacrifice for him. She only knew that he came as requested and then came again.

The visits did not change her mother's view of him. She admitted to herself that he carried himself well, knew his way around a formal sitting room and dining room as well as the men of her city. Still, she did not like him.

Helena's father looked into his daughter's eyes and saw it was hopeless to question her further.

On his fourth visit, Sr. Machado lingered over dessert, then asked Julio if he could speak with him in his library. When they emerged, Helena's father said, "Show Sr. Machado to the front door, my dear one," and left them alone.

Helena took Sr. Machado's hand and led him into the front hall. When they reached the door, he looked down at her, saying nothing. Heat rose in her body, traveled to her face. She glanced down, sure she was blushing. He brushed a few stray hairs off her cheek, tucked them gently behind her ear. Then he lifted her chin so she was once again looking at him, said, "Please call me Roberto," kissed her mouth and left.

She wanted to run after him, kiss him again with lips that were stinging. She wanted to beg him to take her with him now. She stood at the open door until she could no longer see him, until she was left with only the memory of his kiss and the scent of windblown grass.

✦ ✦ ✦

And so Helena's family drove from long before daybreak through the long stretch of barren country and into the evening rain of Esperança, drove to the flat dirt square, now turning to gumbo in the unrelenting deluge. Mud sprang up at them, spattered the heavy fenders of their limousine, sprayed almost to the windows as they moved slowly down the main street.

Julio was familiar with the dirt roads of the outback, used to brown houses on meandering brown streets. Whenever he could, he wandered these roads, alone in the limousine with only his uniformed chauffeur.

He was head of the customs house in the city. Packages were sent from his care to the tiny post offices that doubled as customs points in the limitless land beyond the capital.

He told himself the postal workers needed a visit from time to time to remind them of the seriousness of their work. In truth, he could have sent any of his employees out to look in on the postal workers. He could have sent no one, let the postal workers do what they would with the tan and tattered boxes stamped with pictures of turbaned men riding jeweled elephants or black Madonnas with their black Jesus babies. He could have seen the infrequent packages off by canoe, truck or donkey to the villages in the interior and never thought of them again.

But Julio yearned for random glimpses of a life beyond his own close world.

The need to see, touch, feel, taste everything drove him from the time he was still a boy. Drove him to seek a position everyone thought beneath him. Drove him through arguments with his powerful and wealthy father, who wanted and could buy more for him than head of the customs house, through tearful pleadings from his mother, who hoped her youngest, most tender son would enter the priesthood, through the derisive comments of friends—"So you're going to spend your days taking bribes from greasy ship captains?"—when he was apprenticed to the old man who ran the customs house.

The old man disappeared soon after greeting his new charge. Four months later, a chewed body washed up on a beach far south of the capital city. It was declared to be the old man, murdered in a deal gone wrong.

In fact, no one could be sure if it was someone important or just another unfortunate fisherman washed off his flimsy raft by a flick of God's finger. No matter. Helena's father, young as he was, took over the customs house, hired new inspectors and experienced guards at high wages to keep the old inspectors from killing him.

His family feared for him. But they soon discovered he was protected from harm. His mother said it was Jesus. His father just shook his head at a son apparently so clean no one could touch him. Only the men working with him on both sides of the ocean understood he was not pure. He was as besotted with the riches of the world as the next man. Not money, which meant nothing to him, but the strange and startling, the beautiful and the truly ugly.

"Show me something I haven't seen," he would say. And the importers, thieves and pirates who lived by the sea, would tear off a slat from one crate, lift out a tiny box, and reveal the secret they had saved for him.

On days when nothing in his dusty crates appeased his cravings, when even the bizarre men and wares of the busy harbor began to feel familiar, Julio would command his bewildered, resigned chauffeur to take him through the sparse countryside beyond his city.

Something nameless in the dry air spoke to him as he drove slowly by women with carelessly tied hair, spreading wet clothes to dry in tall grasses at the side of the road, by men in leather breeches and caps, riding herd on white Brahmas with bony humps.

Helena's father had moments when he wanted to stop by the prehistoric-looking cattle, descend from his car and simply stand among them, inhaling their warm breath, leaning against their slender, comforting flanks, stroking their long ears.

He never stopped. Never walked with the cattle, but only gazed from the window, looked at the large, mournful eyes of men and beasts staring at the black limousine intruding in their quiet world.

In villages, children ran alongside the car, shouting and hitting the tires with small sticks. Men, hunkering against mud houses, whistled as he passed. Women looked away, pretending not to notice.

Helena's father was used to that. But, Esperança was different. No one was out in the rain. No children darting by his window in a daring, wet game they had invented; no women crouching in doorways, waiting for the downpour to end; no men anywhere. The town seemed deserted as they pulled up to the brown church settled forlornly, almost inconsolably, on the muddy square.

They sat for one moment, everyone silent, staring as the rain stuttered on the metal roof of the car. Then a small door opened at the side of the church and someone sprinted toward them.

Julio rolled down his window, letting in a shower of water carrying the heavy scent of earth, saw it was a priest running toward them.

The priest, his fresh young face wet and serious, leaned into the car, shouted through the noise of water on the car's metal roof. "No electricity. God's will. Don't worry, many candles have been lit, many candles." Then he ran back into the church, holding his vestments up with one hand to keep the hem out of the mud.

"So the rain has taken your lights," Julio said, looking over at his daughter in the ivory satin gown her mother had worn before her. Helena's veil was laid back from its band of lavender orchids, framing her face like a white halo. Her heavy braid, rolled at the back of her tender neck, was hidden.

She gazed at her father serenely.

"It will be beautiful," she said.

Isabel left the car first, walking quickly through the rain with a grown son on each side of her. When she entered the church, she could see nothing but the flickering flames of the candles placed in tin sconces beside the twelve stations of the cross and perched in niches next to crudely painted carvings of saints.

Smells assailed her, wax from the candles, spicy incense, wet human hair and the odor of rotting earth. She thought she would faint, swayed for a moment as her two sons held tightly to her arms, then shook them off. She knelt quickly on the cold, pounded dirt floor, crossed herself, then strode down the aisle alone toward the Virgin Mary. The Virgin, waiting serenely for her near the altar, was beautiful, obviously a gift from a wealthy family for some past blessing. Her porcelain face was lustrous in the candlelight; her porcelain hands reached out as if to touch Helena's mother.

"Blessed Virgin," Isabel prayed, "guide my child through this dark passage. Lead her into the light, I beg you." She lit a votive candle, placed it in the iron stand with other shimmering votive offerings and turned to take her place in the front pew.

It was only then she realized the church was full. She had been prepared to see no one. Sr. Machado had explained to Julio that his parents were dead, that his cousin was too busy with work on the family plantation to travel to Esperança for the wedding. He would stand alone.

Yet not alone. Faces looked up at Isabel as far back into the gloom as she could see. Men, most of them workers from Sr. Machado's factory, wearing white shirts soft from many washings, their hats resting politely on their knees. Women in print cotton dresses, heads covered with black shawls, brown faces dusted with white powder. Children, quiet and solemn, staring at her. All the eyes were on her, looking at her hair, her face, her city clothes as though fingering them. She sat down quickly, feeling defiled, and began praying again to the Virgin to somehow, miraculously, deliver her child from this horror.

Her husband, standing in the dark at the back of the church, his only daughter at his side, whispered one last question.

"Are you sure?"

"It's what I want."

And so he carefully helped Helena drop the veil over her face, guided her down the aisle toward the man waiting for her, kissed her hand as she left him.

He watched Helena put her arm shyly through Sr. Machado's, who looked larger in this place than he had in the city. As Julio took a step back, Sr. Machado turned and looked into his eyes. There was no gratitude, only acceptance of what was now rightfully his.

Julio groped for the pew, sat heavily between his two sons. In the darkness, head bowed as if praying, his eyes filled with tears.

Chapter 3

✦ ✦ ✦

Long before her family agreed to send Helena to him, Sr. Machado began rebuilding the house he would offer her. In the old days, his family lived on the sugar cane plantation in the wet country downriver from Esperança. They used the village house only as a place to rest or spend the night before riding out to the cattle herds.

Through the generations, the cane thrived and so did the family. Sr. Machado's father, the second son of a second son, assessed his future on the plantation and moved to the village house to run the small ranch. The ground by then was good for nothing, hard clay that choked even weeds and left crops and cattle starving. It was perfect for cement.

Sr. Machado grew up visiting his cousins on the plantation, riding their horses on narrow dirt roads beside green felt fields. But his home was his father's factory.

It had not always been so. There had been a time, when he and his mother were both young, that his world promised more than the gray factory walls of his father, more than the gloom of the village house.

Someone looking at the little boy and his mother might have thought otherwise. But the child Roberto saw only what he could see—a mother he adored who gave him hugs and kisses despite her husband's disapproving looks, who read books to him filled with fanciful drawings of fairies and dragons on days she was not lying in her own dark room, who did not insist that he finish the dull lessons his tutor left every week, who rode a horse better and faster than his father.

It was his mother who ministered to him when his lungs filled in the night and his gasps brought her running to his room, who tenderly applied the stinging, hot poultices to his chest and stroked his hands and forehead until he fell asleep, who asked her husband again and again to let them go to the plantation where the clear air might give their son relief.

Sometimes they would be gone for weeks, sometimes for months. Roberto's father visited but did not stay long. The child and his mother passed whole days on horseback, Roberto trying new, reckless tricks to make his mother laugh out loud. They played hide and seek in the pantry garden, read ancient books of alchemy and witchcraft his mother pulled from cupboards in their bedrooms. They sought the old wisdom of the women who worked in the kitchen and fields and had powers to cure the boy. In dark corners of crumbling adobe huts, the women would bring out dusty powders ground from ancient herbs and flowers, mix black, syrupy teas for Roberto to drink at his mother's gentle coaxing, read the new lines in his small palm to foretell the future of his tender lungs.

Nothing the old women gave Roberto cured him. As they knew it would not. They understood, as the little boy lay in their hammocks or sat at kitchen tables set out under wide-leaved trees, that Roberto must be helped but not healed. To heal him would be to cut him and his desperate mother off from the green air of the plantation. Both would suffer.

And so, for a time, he woke in the night and he gasped. His mother ran to him, unaware and full of love, and then begged her husband for yet another reprieve. For a time, Roberto's father said yes.

And then, one day like any other, he forbade his wife to go. Roberto was sent on alone, despite pleas from his mother that he was too small, too sick. When he returned, several weeks later, his mother was in bed, ill with an unnamed disease, a wasting away. Roberto heard the maids whispering about the "mal vento," the evil wind that had blown through the house on the very hour he was climbing aboard the canoe for his trip to the plantation.

His mother never recovered. She died during the next rainy season, while Roberto was away on yet another stay at the plantation. She had begged him not to go, despite the invitation from his cousins, despite his father's stern reminder that he must learn to be a man, to stand against the whims of his weak mother. He left, not understanding that his world would soon be undone.

The rains were fierce that year. The Rio Branco roared out of its banks like a beast from one of Roberto's fairy books, devoured all the land around its borders. Earth beneath the river, old earth that had not been disturbed since before the time of man, boiled up, claiming its brother soil for its own, taking boulders, houses, dogs and horses, cattle and children into its watery clutch until they were twice drowned. Bodies turned up two hundred kilometers from home, taking the longest journey of their short, sad lives.

Word of Roberto's mother's death reached the plantation in the mouth of a bargeman gathering carcasses of cows and men alike off the devil river's chewed-up banks. By the time Roberto found his way back to Esperança, his father had turned their wedding portrait to the wall and buried her in the sodden ground. Her clothes were gone, her hair brushes and crosses packed into a leather box Roberto found only after his father died.

Her name was never spoken again, as if she had never lived. Roberto was nine.

He and his father began eating breakfast together and then going to the factory. His lungs were forgotten. Despite the gray, sticky air in the factory, his disease disappeared. He began to learn the ways of his father's world. There was no question of him taking over when his father was too old or ill to work. Roberto would inherit the factory, and he would continue to run it as his father had. Work was their link, a hard bond forged in their mutual grief. The only beauty in their lives had disappeared. Roberto's father would lose himself in his work. He would teach his young son to do the same.

After his father died, Roberto closed himself off further. Except for occasional joyous trips to the plantation, now run by his cousins, and occasional nights with one of the young village women—always a different woman and always shown the back way out of the house by the early-rising cook—Roberto did nothing but work. He lived in two small rooms in his village house, took a short daily ride on Ouro Preto, ate his breakfast and supper in the kitchen with the cook.

Looking at the house through the eyes of Helena, he saw for the first time how impoverished his life had become.

He brought three workmen from his factory, men wiry from pouring vats of concrete into molds. None of them had ever been inside his house. They wandered through the warren of bedrooms in the back as he showed them where they should tear out walls, where to build a stairway for the upper story they would add.

As Esperança watched, the house rose to a second floor then rose again with the construction of a small tower at the back. Encased in the same soft yellow plaster as the rest of the house, the tower was said to be for the senhor's bride. It would cure her homesickness, the villagers said, by giving her a view of the sea.

Workers poured a fountain in the factory, hauled it by ox cart to the house and installed it in the inner courtyard. They opened the face of the house and built a vestibule, lined with Portuguese tiles and entered through high gates of wrought iron.

✦ ✦ ✦

The maids, hired from town to tend to Roberto's bride, found her happy in her house, a child playing with new toys. Everything delighted her. The parakeets living in the courtyard, the silver and china hauled in wooden trunks by barge from the capital city, the niche built into the vestibule wall for her statue of the archangel Gabriel, the horse Roberto brought upriver from the plantation so they could take long rides together.

And something else, a look in her eye, a languor in her movements when the tiniest maid, little Carmelinha, brought in her breakfast tray of milky coffee and heavy silver bowl of sugar, that let them know she was learning well the nighttime lessons her master must be teaching her.

In fact, she was teaching him. Roberto, at 32, was experienced in love. As a boy, he had been schooled in the rough games of his uncles' mistresses and scolded by the maids in the plantation house to remember soft words and caresses. The village girls, mostly struck dumb and frightened by a night with him, did whatever he asked. He told himself before he brought Helena home that he must be tender with her, must not frighten her so that she wouldn't take his seed for sons. What no one had prepared him for was her own passion.

Some girls wed themselves to Jesus and vow to live a life as chaste as possible within the duties of marriage. Helena was not one of them. She walked through the cloistered halls of her school like an orchid of the jungle, waiting only for a chance ray from the sun to heat its petals and open up its beauty.

Night after night, she wrapped her white legs around her husband, rocked him gently or rode him as he rode Ouro Preto, found hidden places to kiss and lick him, guided his kisses to her own secrets.

Night after night, the maids living in his house were amazed to hear his cries mingled with his bride's. At dawn, he staggered down the stairs, put on whatever shirt they offered him, mounted Ouro Preto and rode out onto the plain. An hour, two hours later, he'd be back, for a long shower and a hot coffee, fresh clothes while his bride slept sweetly on. It did no good. He was besotted.

At first, the factory workers smiled. But after awhile, his foremen began to grumble among themselves. Their patron couldn't behave this way. To pluck a sweet virgin's flower and revel in her perfume—yes. To languish for a time in her love croonings, better, if you are that lucky. But enough is enough. He is a man, after all.

So everyone breathed a sigh of relief when the maids announced to Esperança that Helena was pregnant. Now she will be a little mother, they said. Now the senhor can find his passion in arms that don't hold him so tightly.

Helena grew big. Her delicious face took on an unearthly quality, not saintly, but focused inward on the baby growing in her. Roberto, overwhelmed by the changes in her body, backed away.

Their son was born on the cool evening of a hot Wednesday. Helena's screams graced the square all that day, in premonition of the nighttime life she and the villagers would later share. Luis was healthy and beautiful, with his mother's eyes and delight in the world. Word went around Esperança that he bore the crown birthmark of royalty.

Sundays that the priest was in town they went to church together. Roberto, not seen in the church since the day he and Helena married, seemed content to walk solemnly past the village eyes, a radiant Helena beside him, her son carried not by a maid, but in her own protective arms.

✦ ✦ ✦

So life continued for six years. The gossiping maids and the village found it strange that no more babies were born. After all, the cries that had echoed through the upstairs hallway still floated on the night air from time to time. Helena still lolled in her bed, her braid unraveled and her mouth soft after her husband had left his bed to ride through a night with her.

Still, no one worried. She was young; she had given him a beautiful son. Life was good. The factory turned out its quota of wash tubs, basins and troughs for the eager patrons in the capital. The villagers worked their long hours without complaint. The fishermen fished and were not often bitten, the canoes swam upriver every week with their school girls, who turned their glossy heads to stare at the small town, rising like a brown topaz out of the dust.

Chapter 4

+ + +

One Monday, the fishermen wading out into deep water and crossing themselves to guarantee a good catch without vicious teeth, were surprised to see one of the school boats slow as it rounded the bend toward them. The motor cut suddenly, the canoe drifting in silence toward the river's edge as the fishermen stood waiting. A plank was thrown over the side of the boat and a young man, dressed in a black suit and starched white shirt, stepped out. His pants were rolled up, and his black polished shoes and thin socks were in his hand. He was sweating in the early morning air. The fishermen could see his collar was very tight.

He walked carefully down the plank as the girls of Nossa Senhora drank in his long, white feet, his slender ankles, the smell of his sweat and citrus cologne wafting over them. He stepped into the shallows of the Rio Branco and ran up the bank. As the motor roared and the canoe slipped into deeper water, the girls saw him sitting on the bank, wiping off his feet with a white handkerchief and putting on his socks.

The school teacher, for he was a teacher, laced up his shoes, picked up his brown suitcase, and walked through town to the front gate of Helena's house.

The word went around the factory the next day. Helena was looking for a companion for her boy, another boy the same age to play and study with him. Helena would interview the boys herself, and choose the one who would stay with her child.

He would live in the yellow house with Helena. He would learn everything her son learned, eat the same food, wear the same proper short pants and hard shoes, speak with the same cultured voice as her son. When Luis was sent away to school, his friend would go with him.

Everything, of course, would be provided for both boys equally.

✦ ✦ ✦

On a hot morning, a line formed at Helena's front gate. The sun was fierce in the sky. Roberto was at his factory. Helena and Sr. Tomás, the school teacher, were seated in the inner courtyard. The cement fountain gurgled and splashed. Helena sat under a small flowering peach tree, the only tree like it anywhere on this flat plain. Her white chair of scrolled iron was decorated with the leaves and fruits of a country she had never seen. The small table beside her was made of the same fantastic iron fruits—pears, cherries, clusters of grapes. She was dressed in a white skirt with a black sash, a black-and-white striped blouse tied with a black ribbon at the high neck. Her braid was pinned in a neat roll at the back of her head.

Sr. Tomás sat in the chair's mate on the other side of the table. He was wearing his black suit and sitting half in the shade of the peach tree and half in the sunlight filtering through the fronds of a banana palm that partially covered the air over the courtyard. A pitcher of fresh lemonade with chipped ice and glasses sat between them on the table. The glasses were for Helena and the young boys she would interview.

Each boy was pulled through the front gate by Carmelinha. Anxious mothers were left outside to fret in the hot dust of Esperança. As the first boy was led back out to the waiting arms of his mama, the next boy was led in, past the archangel Gabriel, through the dark sitting room with its glowing ruby rug and its hulking chairs of carved jacaranda wood and out into the moist sunlight of the courtyard.

The boys stood in front of Helena. She talked to them quietly. She knew how to gentle them as she calmed the tiny birds in her peach tree by stroking their feathers with one small finger until they stared at her, transfixed. She coaxed the boys into telling her everything they saw, thought, played.

Sr. Tomás asked them four questions: What is your full name? How do you spell it? What are the numbers written on this paper? What is the capital city of our state?

Then Helena rang the silver bell placed on an embroidered napkin by the lemonade pitcher. Just before Carmelinha led them out, Helena gave each one a hug.

No matter what their fate in life, whether they ended up fishing and enduring the taunting teeth of the piranhas, whether they left Esperança on a wooden cart laden with sacks of rice and beans, whether they died early or lived to see their babies have babies, they all remembered that embrace.

Late at night, lying in their woven hammocks or their narrow marriage beds with the wedding coverlet of stiff crocheted lace drawn across their chests, they would suddenly be visited by the scent of lilies mixed with something damp and warm, the smell of fresh lemons coming from her mouth, the touch of hair heavy as bread just out of the clay oven.

✦ ✦ ✦

She chose a child no one knew. His parents lived at the edge of Esperança, in a mud hut with no white plaster face to give it substance and status. His father was a fisherman, a man who threw his nets with skill and caught as many fish as other men, but never seemed to sell as many. Their house was on a small bluff overlooking the Rio Branco. One bad spring, before the fisherman had a wife and son, his house had washed away. Other years, the growling water gouged away chunks of the bluff beside their house until it now teetered on the edge of another disaster.

The fisherman had married his young wife in a rush. Five months later, she bore him a healthy son and named him José.

She was a laundress who took underwear, flowered shirts and dresses, heavy cotton sheets to a rocky eddy in the river and washed them. From the other women in the sudsy river water, skirts pulled between their legs and tucked into waistbands to keep the hems from getting wet, she learned about the interviews to take place at Helena's house. She ran home, pulled her son's only white shirt from the small leather trunk where it was folded and ran back to the river to wash the dust and yellow out of it.

A week later, a blue envelope was delivered to the house above the river by a maid from the yellow house. The laundress walked into town carrying the blue envelope carefully in one hand and several mangoes in a net bag in the other. At the mercantile, she gave Dona Ana the mangoes for a reading of the letter.

"Sr. and Sra. Machado invite your son to act as companion and schoolmate to Master Luis. Studies will begin in one week, Monday. Sr. and Sra. Machado await your reply."

Soon everyone in Esperança knew which boy had been chosen. But none knew or could understand why.

Dona Ana herself had sent her son over to be interviewed in Helena's cool courtyard. True, he was older than Luis. But he could already read and write fluently and mind his manners. She had heard from one of the housemaids that Sr. Tomás was very taken with him and held him up to Helena as a good model for her son.

The discussion was in vain. Helena decided on the fisherman's son almost as soon as he walked in. He was smaller than her own son but had a natural grace that she found surprising in a boy born of a fisherman.

As he stood before her, not speaking and head bowed shyly, she said, "Look at me, please," in a quiet voice.

When he didn't move, she reached over, cupped his chin in her hand and lifted up his face. For one moment, he looked directly at her with eyes as dark and mature as a man's. Then he looked down, long black lashes hiding his astonishing eyes and she took her hand away from his face.

Only he did not receive a hug at the end of his interview. She withheld the small gift to offer him the larger one and to keep herself from beginning to spoil him.

She knew she had spoiled her own son, didn't think it wrong. He was gentle enough to withstand her attention without demanding more. But he would need a companion who was stronger, less loved by women. This little boy, although she couldn't say why, showed a determination that tugged at her. She was attracted and fascinated by the flash of force in that one look. She chose him.

Chapter 5

+ + +

José came alone to Helena's house. It was early. His father was braving the muddy Rio Branco. His mother was home weeping for her only son. There was nothing left of him in the brown house by the river. She had sent him out with everything he owned wrapped in the linen sheet she had been saving for her burial shroud. She knew she would not see him again, knew that once he entered Helena's house, he would be hers forever.

He left wearing his white shirt and short pants that his mother had pressed with the charcoal in her iron as hot as she dared. In his sheet, tied with the remnants of one of his father's piranha-chewed nets, he carried a floral shirt made from the leftover scraps of his mother's skirt, her rosary of black beads, a comb, the cream-colored hammock he had slept in since he was a baby.

He arrived carrying his possessions on his small head, hair still wet from his mother's ministrations. He put his bundle down in the dirt and stood shyly at the front gate until Carmelinha came to lead him into his new life.

She took him upstairs, stripped him down and made him climb into a tub of steamy water. She scrubbed his hair with harsh soap, dug under his fingernails with a sharp metal file, scoured his teeth with a brush. She dressed him in a starched white shirt that scratched him, wool shorts that itched, long black socks and hard shoes that made his feet swell in the heat.

His other clothes disappeared, along with the hammock, the comb, the sheet. He was allowed only the rosary.

Through that long day, he saw no one but Carmelinha and the cook. He heard someone laughing once, a boy, he thought. And he felt eyes on him from shadows in the dark house.

◆ ◆ ◆

He sat in the dining room on cushions piled into a chair with huge carved arms. Carmelinha pushed him up to the table and he ate, in silence, rich food he couldn't identify with a silver spoon so heavy he thought he would drop it. Then she led him upstairs, hung a plaid hammock with long fringe in the room she said was his, opened all the windows made of wondrous glass and told him to nap. As he lay in the hammock, making it rock gently by pushing with one small foot against the polished wood floor, he thought he could smell the muddy river where his father fished.

That night, when he climbed into a bed for the first time in his life, he held onto the rosary. Its beads, made of rolled rose petals dried black, still held the faint scent of his mother's hands. He told himself to forget her, as she had said he must.

The next morning, he met Luis. He was led down-stairs in his new clothes, his feet aching, and out into the courtyard. This time, Helena embraced him. Then she brushed back his hair from his forehead, looked into his eyes and told him he would be happy now. He believed her. Whatever happiness was, this beautiful lady would know how to give it to him.

He and Luis were taken away by Sr. Tomás to begin their first lesson together. Through all the days that followed, as José sat with Luis at their little desks in the nursery, he heard Helena speaking to him. It was her voice that echoed in his head as he memorized the sounds of each new letter on Sr. Tomás' hand-held blackboard, her voice that told him the answers to the addition problems when Roberto quizzed the boys at night.

Their father would be waiting, hands on his knees, in the scrolled dining room chair where he always ate his supper, as the two boys were brought in by Sr. Tomás. They sat on small stools at his feet and recited what they had learned that day. Then they were led out, to have their soup in the kitchen where Roberto had once taken his lonely meals.

As the lessons progressed from addition to subtraction, from letters to words to sentences, José saw that he was learning faster than Luis. This surprised him. He had assumed that the people in the big house not only had more money and paler skin but were smarter. They did know things he didn't—where to find a cloth as light as breath and another heavy as the water where his fisher father pulled his nets, how to grow a tree that produced wondrous pink globes, how to capture the light of the sun in tiny bursts that hung from each ceiling in the house.

They knew how to grow tall and straight with narrow feet and white teeth. Luis, still as beautiful as his mother, was growing faster than José, as if life with his small friend had given him courage. He was able to mount his pony on his own, while José still needed a boost from Sr. Tomás.

Once in the saddle, though, José was fearless. Luis guided his pony gently around the ring of wooden stakes Roberto had driven into the hard earth behind the house, gravely giving the horse precise instructions by tapping it on the neck with his guide stick. José smacked his pony on the flanks with the stick, making it gallop and rear until Helena and all her maids would scream at him to stop.

In the nursery, he was just as daring. Sr. Tomás, torn between duty to his mistress and a chance to show off his own teaching skills, still knew he had to hold José in check. José soon learned to keep some of his sums and new words to himself.

So the days passed. Sr. Tomás took the boys away to the nursery every morning after breakfast, where their mouths had been wiped by Helena herself. Lunch was in the courtyard or in the dining room with the heavy chandelier of crystal flames, the carved jacaranda table with its lace runner and glass vinegar and oil cruets set into a basket of woven silver.

The table, a wedding gift from Roberto's cousins, sat for generations in the plantation house dining room. Its high polish still bore the scars of rough men sitting down to their meat with machetes in their sashes, children kicking its legs with their riding boots, coffins slid onto the bare wood for mournful wakes.

Many of Roberto's relatives had taken their final rest on this table, their mahogany coffins open so that the family could kiss them, caress their sunken cheeks and pluck faded roses off their pillows, have photographs taken of the living with the dead to remind them of their last hours together.

Roberto came home at noon to large, elaborate meals of fish stew or shrimp boiled in coconut milk followed by shredded beef with rice and beans and then a doce—angel kiss meringues in sugar syrup or huge macaroons and a hot cafezinho.

Luis and José, perched on their cushions, were allowed to eat their doce before Roberto and leave the table. But they usually stayed, begging cook for another meringue and watching their father finish his meal. Linen napkin tucked into his white shirt, black hair combed straight back from his high forehead, he would lean over his plate, piling beans, farinha, rice and diced tomato onto the back of his fork. When his food was gone, he would call to the kitchen maid to bring another piece of the charbroiled beef.

The boys were fascinated by the amount of food he ate. For Luis, it was a question of pride. For José, it was a matter of daily wonder. Even after he grew accustomed to the foods on the table in front of him, he couldn't imagine one person needing so much. The fact that Roberto never got fat was beyond José's knowledge. There had never been a fat man in Esperança.

After lunch, the maids unrolled the hammocks from their wall hooks. On sunny days, Roberto rested in the courtyard. The boys went to their rooms. Helena, growing up in the city, didn't use a hammock. She lay down on a bed with fresh sheets.

The fan of painted wood turning gently overhead was the only sound in the room, in the house, in the town. Nothing else stirred. The great paddles of Roberto's cement mixers were stopped, their buckets cleaned and scraped. The men at the factory hung like delicate cocooned moths in their hammocks slung between their huge machines. The parakeets in Helena's courtyard were still, heads tucked under their jeweled feathers. The frogs, whose voices echoed through the dark nights of the land beyond Esperança, lay deep and silent in their muddy water holes. The world stopped while Helena rested.

Chapter 6

✦ ✦ ✦

One afternoon a week, the boys had catechism training from Helena. Young Father Simon had granted permission for them to receive their training at home. He was in Esperança only one Sunday a month, while traveling the back roads between Ilha das Flores and Mariana on a smoke-belching commercial bus with the eyes of Jesus painted on the front. He usually arrived at Esperança's grandly named Gloria de Todos os Santos church nauseous from gas fumes and late for his frantic schedule of services, confessions, baptisms, weddings.

Sometimes he was met at the bus by the church caretaker with a litany of complaints. The Gloria roof sprung leaks in creative places—directly into the baptismal font which sprang its own sympathetic leak, over the crucifix where it ran down the face of Jesus, giving rise to the rumor that the Savior was crying miraculous green tears.

Sometimes the caretaker had made arrangements for a funeral, if the death was late in the week and the weather was cool. Other Sundays, there would be prayers to be said over the dead in new graves dug in the dry earth behind the church.

Father Simon was happy to let Roberto instruct the boys at home, although he did allow himself one private, intense moment of regret. He could see himself seated at the Machados' heavy table where he had planned Luis' christening not so long ago. He was eating a sugary meringue and drinking in the sight of Helena speaking sweetly to him and only him about the life of the Virgin Mary. He sighed, let the vision fade and gave Roberto his blessing.

Roberto tried one impatient half-hour lesson with the boys and then passed the honor of catechism training to his wife whose instruction from the nuns of Escola de Nossa Senhora was impeccable.

✦ ✦ ✦

Every Tuesday afternoon, while Luis and José were still drowsy from their naps, Helena met the boys in the nursery. She sat in front of them on a small padded chair taken from her bedroom. They sat at their school desks, knees together, hands folded on the desk tops. Both tried to concentrate on the words of the Lord, remembering the stern admonition from Sr. Tomás to sit perfectly still when Helena was teaching them. He knew well enough how they wriggled even when the subject was the anatomy of the horse. God, in hour-long segments, would be a large dose for two small boys to swallow.

But José grew to love the weekly lessons with Helena. For the first time since he had shyly entered her gates, he could look directly at her when she asked him a question.

He could listen to the low voice that was always in his head, breathe the same air she breathed.

"Who made us?" Helena would ask.

"God made us."

"Who is God?"

"God is the Supreme Being, infinitely perfect, who made all things and keeps them in existence."

Every week, the boys memorized the answers to Helena's questions. Every Tuesday, she repeated questions from earlier lessons and added new questions. If Luis faltered, and it was always Luis, she reminded him gently that he must respond quickly and well to shine in God's eyes and not embarrass his mama.

Luis would furrow his handsome brow and try harder. José would sit in his little chair that matched Luis' and wish that, just this once, he could answer for Luis. He wanted to shine in God's eyes too. He wanted to shine for Helena.

On a particularly lazy Tuesday afternoon, when the children and Helena slept longer than usual and the sun seemed hot enough to melt the windows and scorch flies on the blazing glass, she began the fourth lesson of the catechism.

"The chief creatures of God are angels and men. God created the angels to see, love and adore Him in heaven," she read. "All the angels were put on trial by God, as we are now being tried so that we may gain heaven. Some of the angels sinned. These are the bad angels, or devils in hell, who tempt to sin."

When she had finished reading, Helena closed the catechism without asking them to memorize the questions and told the surprised boys to follow her. She led them out of the nursery, down the stairs and into the cool, dark vestibule. They stood in front of the terrible statue who lived there.

"Today, I want to tell you the story of my angel," Helena said. Luis tipped his head back to look up at his mama's angel. José stared at the hem of his robe.

"This is the archangel Gabriel. He is a messenger from God. He came to the blessed Virgin Mary to tell her that she would bear the son of God. He came to me when I was very young, younger than you are now."

Gabriel loomed over the boys, wings pushed forward as though still in flight, long curls sweeping the air in front of his small, fierce face. He looked as though he were rushing to give news that would break someone's heart, José thought. Rushing to hand someone a small, blue envelope. "Sr. and Sra. Machado invite your son to act as companion and schoolmate to Master Luis."

"One day," Helena began, "a woman came to our gate. She was the honey brown of a roasted cashew and wearing a dress the color of dust. On her head, she carried a heavy burden wrapped in burlap. She looked like a beggar woman, except for her sash. It was white silk, with red and gold threads embroidered into the shapes of flowers that have no names.

"'You have a special child,' the woman said to my mother. 'I will make a figure for her, a statue of her guardian angel. He will protect her and guide her.'"

Helena's mother had not wanted to open her gate to the strange woman, was ready to tell her, "We are feeding many people here. We have nothing for you," when she looked into the woman's eyes. Blue eyes in a brown face, eyes like the sky after a rain when the color has bled into the ocean. Looking into those eyes, Isabel glimpsed her own future. She saw herself inviting this strange woman into her house, making a bed for her on a dirt floor, bringing her cold soups and hot teas, telling her goodbye with relief when the woman's mysterious work was done.

"I am Nilsa. Let me in," the woman said. Her voice was low and powerful. Despite her poor appearance, she sounded like a woman who was given what she needed. Isabel was afraid to turn her away. She opened the gate to her and led her without thought to the gardener's shed by the back courtyard. The small room with one shuttered window housed a bench for the gardener's tools and a jumble of bicycles and bird cages and bamboo rakes.

Nilsa stepped into the shed and took a slow, deep breath. She filled her lungs with the smell of rich dirt in old clay pots, roots and seeds buried in stone jars for next year's planting.

"This is the place," she said.

She directed everything to be removed but the wide bench. She asked only for a mattress, which was brought in and laid on the pounded dirt floor.

"From deep in her burlap bundle," Helena said to Luis and Jose, "she pulled a black velvet coverlet sprinkled with half-moons and stars in white satin. Tiny silver amulets hung from some of the star points—a hand, a woman's torso, a lightning rod, a heart, an arrow tipped with red, an eye with a yellow topaz pupil, lips parted by a protruding tongue, a kidney, a foot.

"She spread the coverlet over the mattress, smoothed it carefully, and said, 'Now I am ready to begin. Bring the child to me.'

"My mother found me in my bedroom, playing with my china doll.

"'Don't say a word,' she told me.

"I followed her into the shed, hid behind her skirt when Nilsa said, 'Come here.'

"When I wouldn't come, she shrugged and began pulling lumps wrapped in white cheesecloth from her sack."

Nilsa unwound the long strip of cloth from the first piece of clay as if removing a bandage from a misshapen head and set it on the bench. The clay was not brown like the dirt of the city, but a lighter shade of her own face and arms, as though it had been taken from her body. She took more clay from her bag, mounding it high. She began molding the clay, working it with her strong fingers. Her fingernails glowed white in the light coming through the open door of the shed.

Helena, drawn toward the hands with the luminous nails, moved away from her mother. Nilsa saw the little girl was captured and reached for her. Isabel tried to grab the sleeve of Helena's dress. But Nilsa pulled her quickly away by her left hand, which she pressed into the clay.

"See how cool it is," she said. "It will warm to you. It will live for you."

She turned to Isabel.

"Tea," she demanded. "Hot and strong. I have been walking long days to come to you."

Isabel took Helena's free hand and turned as if in a dream, obeying this woman she did not know. Mother and daughter went into the kitchen.

"You must not go in there alone and you must not speak to her," Isabel said as she set a pan of water over the stove's flame. "She wants you."

Her words were fearful but not strong enough to break Helena's fascination. When Isabel took the tea to the shed, Helena followed, amazed to see her mother carrying the pot herself instead of calling for a maid to take it out.

The shed door was closed. Isabel crossed herself and set the small teapot with its vining roses on the ground by the door. Nilsa would know the tea was there, would know when Isabel left without hearing her go.

"I had a dream last night of the blue eyes," Isabel said to Helena the next morning as she was brushing her daughter's hair. "Blue eyes in a brown face are gypsy magic. Be very good while she is here. Pray hard for your soul so that her work will protect you. Her magic can be used for good or evil."

Little Helena prayed that night, like every night, for her brothers, her mother and father. She prayed for God to take her soul into heaven to be with her grandmother Clara and her baby sister. And then, kneeling at her bedroom altar with her saints and the blessed Virgin, she prayed earnestly and with her hands pressed tightly together not to be taken, to be spared the magic of the gypsy woman if it meant leaving her mother and father and flying to heaven.

Every morning, Helena and her mother made hot tea for the gypsy. After several days, Isabel saw that the shed door stayed closed and let Helena carry the teapot to the shed.

"It will be good for her to see your kindness," she said. "She will feel love for you."

Afternoons, Helena carefully carried out plates of fruit and small pieces of chicken or crab her mother saved from the noon meal. Sometimes, Isabel placed a flower on the plate, but never any red meat.

"It inflames the soul," she said.

At night, Isabel sent Helena out in her white nightgown to retrieve her teapot and plate. The teapot was always empty, but the plate of food was often untouched. One night, Helena took the full plate to her bedroom. She prayed to her saints and the Holy Virgin to rock her gently through the dark and lead her on toward morning. Then she climbed into her bed with the forbidden plate and took small bites of Nilsa's food—cold roasted chicken with lime, mango miraculously fresh hours after being cut.

"That was the first night I heard the music," Helena told the boys. "When it began, long after dark, I didn't realize who it was. It was like no music I had ever heard, no human voice. I hear it now whenever I'm near my Gabriel. It is a flute on the wind, or the air itself, moving in and out of God's pure throat."

The next morning, little Helena told her mother about the beautiful music.

"No one's singing," Isabel said.

◆ ◆ ◆

Two mornings later, the maid who watered the courtyard trees ran into the kitchen, shouting "Madre mia," and crossing herself.

"She's turned herself into the devil," she screamed at Isabel and sat down on the floor, moaning.

Isabel gathered the other maids around her and crossed the courtyard to the open shed door. Peering into the blackness with the circle of women, Helena glimpsed only a small, wild face. After a moment, her eyes adjusted to the dark, and she saw she was staring at an angel with upraised wings and flying skirts.

"Dear God," Isabel said. "It's Gabriel."

The gypsy was gone and everything with her—the coverlet, the white bandages, every morsel of clay. Only the bare mattress lay forgotten in one corner. Helena crept to it and touched the ticking. It was still warm, as though Nilsa had risen from her sleep only moments before and pressed what was left of herself into the soft body of Gabriel.

"She came to us through dreams. Now she's disappeared like the devil's smoke," Isabel said. She shuddered, grabbed Helena's arm and yanked her to her feet.

"You're not to come back in here," she said. "Ever."

The gardener carried Helena's messenger of tidings into the courtyard to harden in the sun. When Gabriel was dry, Isabel, afraid of his gaze, had him returned to the shed and locked the door with the rusty slide bolt.

"At night, I sometimes heard him singing," Helena said. "But I didn't see him again until my parents sent my belongings to this house. They were right. He was meant to come here."

She lifted Luis up to kiss Gabriel. Then she lifted José. He felt his feet leaving the tile floor, felt Helena's slender fingers gripping his waist. He gazed into the fearsome face of her archangel, kissed his mad hair, and was lowered gently to the comforting earth.

CHAPTER 7

+ + +

ON SUNNY AFTERNOONS when the boys had no cate-chism lesson, they were taken out under the watchful eye of the cook or a maid to ride their ponies or kick a soccer ball behind the house. Those afternoons, Helena and Sr. Tomás painted.

The painting lessons began as a request from Sr. Tomás. Would Helena mind the smell of paint in his room? And could he order oils and small canvases from the city? They would take no space, and he would not paint anything offensive.

Several weeks later, Dona Ana's son, the same son who had come to petition for a place in Helena's home and heart, stood again at her gate. This time, he carried a heavy box wrapped in brown paper and tied with string. The box, bearing the names of both Sr. Machado and Sr. Tomás, had traveled upriver from the capital city on the school canoe. It had been transported from the river bank to Dona Ana's mercantile by a fisherman down on his luck. He had traded delivery of the box for two cigarettes from Dona Ana.

She would not request reimbursement from Sr. Machado. Her son would refuse anything but a small glass of water from Carmelinha. He would drink the water in the cool vestibule under the glaring eye of the archangel Gabriel. The favor would be noted by Helena and by the heavens. Recompense, it was assumed, would come when it was most needed.

Carmelinha brought the box of paints, with its odor of linseed oil and turpentine seeping through the wrapping paper, into the kitchen where Helena and the cook were grating coconut meat to make cakes for the midday meal. The bouquet of fresh coconut was strong in the air. But Helena smelled the box before Carmelinha set it down on the narrow kitchen table, recognized a scent from her past. She wiped her hands on her heavy linen apron, picked up the box with the stamp Os Olhos de Michelangelo, and said, "I will take care of this."

She climbed the stairs with her treasure, walked past the nursery where Sr. Tomás was giving Luis and José a geography lesson. Helena heard the low voice of the teacher asking, "What mountain reaches highest into our father's heavens?" and the boys' piping answer in unison.

She continued down the hall and into Sr. Tomás' dark bedroom. She moved without thinking to his desk, the small rosewood desk she herself had used as a child, set the package on top of a pile of papers and books and then leaned over it. She inhaled deeply, drinking in the perfume of her childhood.

◆ ◆ ◆

Os Olhos de Michelangelo was an art supply house, one of many shops along the city's docks. On days when there were no ships in the harbor waiting like pregnant whales to be relieved of their precious cargo, Julio and his young daughter would explore the docks.

Some of the stores were little more than stalls with heavy-based kerosene lanterns hanging from hooks along one wall, fishing nets looped over iron rings on the opposite wall, lavender and green glass floats arranged along the front counter.

Others, proper stores with metal curtains that rolled down at night, displayed the fruits of sea voyages for buyers to take by the basketful to shops in the city. Brilliant red and green India silks, shot through with gold, sand dollars that looked to Helena like the pressed sugar cookies her mother made at Christmas, amber scotch in bottles with wire mesh to protect the glass when ships slid sideways on the swollen sea, ceramic beads the colors of striped lemon and horehound drops, wooden spears wrapped in leather thongs, azure earthenware jars filled with jasmine tea and stoppered with large corks.

The closed world of Helena's childhood, a childhood filled with her mother's daily prayers, tears and rules, opened magically every time she put her hand into her father's and let him lead her onto the boardwalk.

Os Olhos de Michelangelo was her favorite shop. She wandered the aisles without tiring, small head tipped back to see the tall racks of brushes that were wide as a horse's tail or narrow as a cat's whisker. She longed over tiny water-color boxes with their hinged trays for mixing the emeralds, topazes and aquamarines glowing inside, the miniature collapsing brushes and folding water cups small enough for her own hand.

While her father passed the time with Michelangelo's shopkeeper in the back, she ran her fingers secretly over fragile rice papers and mulberry papers the weight of velvet. One day, she found a corner of rose petal paper curling on the dusty wooden floor of the shop. It had been torn away when a busy clerk slid the new paper shipment into narrow shelves. She picked up the scrap with its one perfect petal trapped in fibers, held it to her nose. It gave off the subtle fragrance of fresh flowers and straw warmed by the sun.

Helena knew she was doing something wrong when she slipped the fragment into the lace-trimmed pocket of her white pinafore. She also knew it was hers. It was the first time she stole. After that, her baby hand reached out often for the small prizes Michelangelo offered—a tiny egg of yellow marble, a gray-blue cube of clay with someone's thumb print pushed into one side. Sometimes, Julio gently removed the pilfered goods from her fist or pocket. More often, he offered to pay out of her hearing. The owner of Michelangelo always refused the money, saying, "She will be an artist, senhor."

It was only as an adult that she understood the gift her father had offered her. Not scraps of colored paper and squares of soft clay but the world itself. Anything she desired could be hers. It was an idea her mother would have abhorred, excessive and wanton. It was the secret light of Julio's life, a secret he shared only with his daughter.

Helena came to the docks as often as her mother would let her go. She lived through Julio's eyes, gazing at the precious and dangerous wonders brought to his doorstep, until the day she boarded the canoe for Escola de Nossa Senhora.

That day, her father cried.

✦ ✦ ✦

Now, standing in Sr. Tomás' bedroom, it was Helena's turn to mourn. She stroked the fragrant package from Os Olhos de Michelangelo longingly, looked up with eyes accustomed to the dark and discovered she was staring at a naked man pinned to a large spoked wheel.

Helena stepped back abruptly, almost knocking over the desk chair piled high with books, then leaned over the desk again, entranced by the drawing of the naked man. What she had first taken for spokes, she now saw were two additional arms extending like wings from the man's shoulders, two additional legs spread-eagled out from his hips. His face, handsome and stern, surrounded by flowing curls, seemed Christ-like.

There was a signature on the drawing, Helena saw, half-expecting it to be Sr. Tomás' own. Leonardo da Vinci. A name from posters hanging on the walls of Os Olhos de Michelangelo. *Mona Lisa* was da Vinci's, the beautiful *Mona Lisa*. She resided near the front of the store, gazing down serenely from a wall hung with small tapestries that the owner of Michelangelo had collected on his travels as a young man, when he still had dreams of being an artist.

Helena's father sometimes studied the tapestries, asking the owner about the weaving technique on one, the shining thread on another. Helena always walked to the *Mona Lisa* when she entered Os Olhos de Michelangelo, raising her small face heavenward just to make sure the kind lady's expression had not changed.

The store had one other da Vinci, a copy of *The Last Supper*. Helena could still see it in her mind, Christ sitting with outstretched hands at the covered table, reaching to shield his disciples from the pending betrayal and death.

Sr. Tomás' da Vinci man, pushing with hands and feet to the edge of his imprisoning circle, this man she had never seen.

Sr. Tomás' desk held other wonders—a photograph of two young men grinning and leaning into the camera with their arms over each other's shoulders, a chart of the heavenly bodies, a shaded drawing of seven beautiful young women wearing billowing skirts that seemed to be sewn with bursts of light.

What sort of man is this, Helena thought, who clutters his desk, my desk, with drawings of nude men and women wearing skirts of light? She turned away from the desk and faced the bedroom of Sr. Tomás.

Sunlight sifting through the shuttered window gave the room a hazy, golden tint. The walls wavered in the shimmering light, shifted in and out of focus as if under water. Helena went to the narrow bed, only then noticing that it had been pulled out from the corner. The teacher could lie in his bed and look directly out of his window into the night sky. She ran her fingers over a crocheted bed cover she didn't recognize, one she knew had been made by a woman's hand. The cover seemed to give off heat from his body.

Helena crossed the small room without knowing she was moving. Her fingers, burning, sought the cool silk paisley dressing gown hanging from a hook on an open door of his wardrobe. She stroked it lightly, pulled at the other door. Shelves with two white shirts folded neatly, a green glass bottle with a silver stopper, a tortoiseshell brush and comb. Her nostrils filled with the spicy scent of citrus and something else, unnameable but as familiar as the teacher's black shoes and long, white hands. She buried her face in his dressing gown, rubbed it slowly over her eyelids and lips, then carefully closed the wardrobe doors and started out of the room just as Sr. Tomás walked in.

They almost collided. For a long moment, neither spoke.

"The package," Helena said. "I meant to..." She stopped, saw Sr. Tomás was looking down at her with a smile just visible in one corner of his mouth.

"Teach me to paint," she said.

CHAPTER 8

✦ ✦ ✦

WITH ROBERTO'S PERMISSION, Helena and Sr. Tomás began their painting lessons. Helena knew her husband would consent. He denied Helena nothing. She asked for little beyond the occasional shipments of cloth—dark faille for her Sunday dresses, suede for riding breeches, lawn for her many nightgowns.

She wore nothing frivolous except her nightgowns. From her earliest days, her mother had taught her to "dress like a nun in the daylight and a queen at night." She admonished her, on nights baby Helena did not want to bathe or change out of her dirty pinafore, that she must always be scrubbed clean before sleep and wear a just-laundered white nightgown in case the Lord decided to take her before morning. As she grew older, Helena understood it might not be only God her mother was talking about. It was the closest Helena's mother ever came to discussing relations between husband and wife.

After she married, Helena continued to instruct her seamstress to keep her dresses plain and her nightgowns decorated with satin ribbons and French lace ordered from the city. She wore a fresh nightgown every night whether her husband would be with her or not.

Their nights together had dwindled since the birth of Luis. At first, Helena was not alarmed. She understood, from listening to the maids talking in her mother's house and in her own, that he would retreat from her for a time when she was carrying a child. But she had assumed once Luis was safe in his nursery crib, cared for by his own nursemaid, that she and her husband would resume the heated night life they had shared.

Roberto did come back to her, down the hallway without candle or announcement to stand at the foot of her bed. Some nights, they were lovers as before. Some nights, she carried worry for her child into her bed, though Luis was a good baby, almost never fussy. Some nights, Roberto seemed to hesitate, as though the vision of Helena as his son's mother had forever changed the way he looked at her. As though everything about her body, its shape, even its fragrance, was foreign to him.

More and more, he stayed away. And then, one evening at supper, he told her he would be leaving.

"I'm needed at the plantation," he said. "I should be gone a week, maybe two."

Helena had made one brief trip to the plantation in the months after her wedding. There she met her husband's cousin, Teresa, who ran the plantation, two of Teresa's sons and her grandbaby Sibella. Helena had seen and heard nothing on the trip to make her think her husband was needed there.

She felt as if she had been slapped, that his leaving was a rebuke somehow, an acknowledgment that the world of the yellow house—the world of Helena and Luis— was not enough. She saw her herself alone, as alone in the yellow house as the house itself at the dry edge of endless land.

She could not imagine a night in the house without him. She could not tell him to stay. And so they sat in the waxy light of the dining room's chandelier, and she asked him only once, "Must you go?"

He looked up from his plate.

"There are decisions to be made, Helena," he said carefully, as though speaking to a child. "Teresa is a good manager, but some decisions must be made by the men of the family."

That was all. He went back to his meal.

✦ ✦ ✦

It was only after he had gone to the plantation and returned many times that she began to guess what might draw him away. There was never a message sending for him, no boatman walking through the dusty town bearing a letter, no small boy running through the streets with the words hot on his tongue and a vision of the shiny coin already cool in his hand.

No one asked her husband to come to the plantation. No one needed to.

Roberto carried in his head the figures from the cement factory, vats produced per day, tubs and troughs poured and barged out, money sent in. But his heart held the knowledge of the plantation, its monthly and yearly rhythms of planting, harvesting and shipping, its thick ribbon of sugar flowing out from field to mill to kettle to kitchen. He would get up on a day like any other in Esperança and understand, without question, that he must pack a small valise and go.

He understood all that and one other thing. He knew that, from time to time, he went when he did not have to go.

He left eagerly, stayed away a little longer than he planned. He came back humming, bounced Luis up and down on his knee, gave him rides on his shoulders "like the ponies at the plantation." He always came to Helena's room the first nights after his return. She would meet him at her door, taste his sweetgrass breath and lead him to her waiting bed.

Later, she would snap awake in a panic, slide out of her bed, leaving her sleeping husband behind, and fly down the hall to her beloved son. She must kiss Luis, even if it disturbed his sleep, to see for herself that he had not suffered from her carelessness, that he was still breathing his miraculous breath. She would creep back to her room, promising she would not abandon him again.

And she would not. For days or weeks at a time, Luis would be Helena's every thought, every bite of food she ate, every song and prayer. Then her husband would leave her and come home again, smelling of green rain and tender shoots. She would unbutton his white shirt, feel the pulse of his quiet earth and be lost to her son again.

◆ ◆ ◆

So it was with her painting. She was captivated by the silver tubes with tiny caps arranged in their wooden stalls in Sr.

Tomás' box, entranced by the sensuous names written in flowing letters down the side—alizarin crimson, cadmium yellow, cerulean blue, burnt sienna, raw umber. With the first stroke of color on her pure canvas, she released a longing she had not known was in her.

Everything became a subject for her greedy eye—a shiny red basket in Luis' room filled with brightly-painted wooden toys, a blue pottery bowl of oranges waiting on the kitchen table to be sliced for a rice salad, the tiny jeweled birds in her courtyard, where she set up her own easel and coaxed out Sr. Tomás in his hot black suit. They would sit most of the afternoon. Or she would sit and he would bend to her, getting little done on his own canvas, because of her questions.

She had taken drawing at Nossa Senhora, to develop an eye for the natural beauty of God's world. But the nuns pronounced painting too frivolous, too fraught with a sinful past, to be appropriate for the tender students of their school.

Helena had no thought for the nuns as she bent to her paints.

✦ ✦ ✦

On a sultry afternoon, the boys out riding, Helena challenged herself to paint one perfect peach blossom. Her tree in the courtyard, for it was hers, was in full bloom. She thought first of painting the whole tree, extravagant bursts of palest pink to deepest salmon covering the dark branches she envisioned on her canvas.

But no. God would not be pleased. Excess would not serve her well. She must remember, as always, to temper her wish for too much. She must learn to paint one blossom, one blossom at a time. If she could master a blossom, then she could move on to two blossoms. By the end of her life, perhaps, she would have mastered her brushes well enough to bring the tree to life.

She sat down at her iron table, the wooden easel beside her propping up her canvas, and opened the box of paints. The smell of the silver tubes was exciting to her, a promise of something more beautiful than she had ever seen.

It was that very longing that must be checked. She had once created something as beautiful as God almighty. God had looked on her work, had seen her adoration of her perfect son, and admonished her by giving her no more babies. To ask for another creation as perfect as Luis would be tempting the universe. She made the sign of the cross, sketched in her blossom on the blank canvas, squeezed a small amount of paint onto her palette.

The curving petals took form as if she were plucking them from the tree and laying them gently onto her canvas. She was not painting alone. Her hand was guided by someone else, the master artist himself layering the colors which smelled not of oil, but of the essence of peach. She was afraid to stop, knew that if she put down the brush the moment would be gone.

She painted through the late afternoon hours, with no idea that time was passing. Preciosa, the most iridescent of her small birds, did not sing, but sat in his bamboo cage looking at her with cocked head. No breeze ruffled her. Sr.

Tomás disappeared, although he still sat in the other iron chair, working on a painting of the long canoe that had brought him to Esperança.

Helena thought nothing, felt nothing. She was only an arm, a hand attached to a brush that moved to dip its tiny tongue into the tastes on her palette—slivers of gold, razor slashes of crimson, apricot gauze the color of early morning ocean air.

She painted until the blossom was finished. Luis and José had come in from their ride, been bathed together in the tub by Carmelinha. Roberto would be home soon for his supper of coffee, yellow cheese and bread. The boys were in the kitchen having their evening soup when Helena took one last stroke, like the final sigh and stretch after lovemaking, and put down her brush.

Sr. Tomás was standing over her. His right hand moved toward her as if to touch her shoulder, wake her from her dream. He stared at the painting.

The peach blossom bloomed out from the canvas, the petals curling up from the pistil in a strong heat or supplication, the dark green leaves framing the flower like a deep cushion. He couldn't imagine where the painting had come from. This was beyond what he knew or could create. He glanced at her face, found it drained.

She did not eat supper that night, protected Sr. Tomás from her husband's possible questions by saying only that she was tired after an afternoon in the courtyard. She went to bed and dreamed of petals.

CHAPTER 9

✦ ✦ ✦

IT WAS ROBERTO who suggested Helena paint a family portrait, "a picture of me with my boys."

The plantation house was filled with portraits of his ancestors, long-limbed men dressed in heraldic gear, mounted on rearing horses or standing with hunting dogs none of them had ever owned, long-necked women with ruby lips and searing eyes under thick eyebrows, looking uncomfortable in their high-collared dresses and satin-bowed shoes.

All were painted by itinerant artists who stayed through the rainy winter and decorated the walls of the salon with murals of angels and cherubs and saints and the upstairs sitting rooms with prowling leopards, placid elephants and cool lagoons to temper the heat of drowsy afternoons on the plantation.

None of the portraits had made the journey to the village house. Roberto owned the wedding photograph of his father and mother that hung, as it had since the day his father died, on the wall opposite his single bed. The rest of his walls, and the walls of the entire house, were white and bare.

Once her husband made the request, Helena could not sleep for thinking about the portrait. It would be large, hung in the dining room behind the heavy chair where her husband sat to listen to the boys recite their day's lessons. She would paint him in that same chair, with his sons on either side of him.

She could see the children in her mind, Luis, strong legs planted firmly beside the chair's leg, leaning over one carved arm toward his father and gazing at him with affection, José standing straighter, one small hand resting on the chair arm a little tentatively, as if not sure how close he should venture. He, like Roberto, would be looking directly at the viewer.

Helena could not imagine herself painting such a portrait. But after her experience in the courtyard with her peach tree, she knew she would not paint alone. A higher power would be at work through her. She would dedicate the portrait to the Maker himself.

Sr. Tomás began preparing her for the ordeal. He must take care not to tax her physically, must hold her to a few afternoon hours of lessons every day. On her own, he knew, she would paint herself into exhaustion.

The teacher sent for books from the capital, books so large and expensive they were transported from the river barge by donkey rather than trusting the maids to carry them to the house. The books were old, ordered from the university library where Sr. Tomás himself had studied. They were wrapped in white cotton quilting and shipped with great reluctance. Because they could not be exposed to sunlight or dust, they were carefully stacked in a dark corner of the dining room by Sr. Tomás.

On an ordinary afternoon of an ordinary day, Luis and José sat at the kitchen table stringing boiled peanuts onto thread. The cook, mindful of their fingers tentatively probing with large needles the softest spots of the brown nuts, hovered between the necklace-making and her black pot of spicy pumpkin soup simmering on the stove.

Roberto was in his factory, idly watching the vats of concrete stirring lazily below his office perch. Sr. Tomás and Helena were cocooned in the dark dining room, held in the circle of soft light from the chandelier. Except for the boys chirping in the kitchen, the house was quiet.

Helena and her teacher sat facing each other across the dining table. Sr. Tomás laid back the gold-scrolled leather cover of the book he had chosen for her lesson, a book as ornate as some of the coffins that had found shelter on the same table. He wiped his long hands on a white handkerchief and began gently turning pages as thick and supple as old linen.

Helena, inhaling the musty fragrance of the book as if taking in the breath of the master artists themselves, looked not at the paintings drifting slowly by her, but at the bowed head of Sr. Tomás. His light brown hair, silky as Luis' hair, shone. One lock fell over his pale forehead. His part was white, as though never exposed to harsh sunlight.

She gazed at the top of his head tenderly, as an image rose in her mind—her hand, pushing the lock of hair back with her fingers, laying her palm on his forehead as if tending one of her boys in illness.

Sr. Tomás smoothed a page and looked up at her. She glanced quickly down at the painting he had chosen as he turned the book around so it was facing her.

"Do you know this work?" he asked.

She shook her head. Certainly she knew the subject. Christ, in the center of the painting, his eyes closed and his hands folded, receiving baptismal water from his cousin, St. John. Two small angels knelt to his right. Over his head, a dove descended from the loving, outstretched hands of God.

"I started here, with this painting," Sr. Tomás said. "Or rather, with this angel." His hand rested on the page in front of Helena.

"This is where I met Leonardo da Vinci. The piece is by Verrocchio. But the angel is by Leonardo, who was his apprentice. It is said that when Verrocchio saw what his apprentice had created, he wept and was never able to paint again."

"This angel brought you to your art," Helena said. Her fingers moved over the young face.

"Such as it is. And introduced me to my master Leonardo."

"You didn't know about him before you came to university?"

"I was not educated until I arrived in your city," he said a little stiffly, and Helena saw his embarrassment.

"Please tell me how you came to university," she said.

"It's a simple story. I'll tell you while you sketch the angel God meant for you." He handed her a pencil, his fingers brushing hers lightly, perhaps absently. She studied the small angel looking in adoration at Christ.

And Tomás began his story.

"I was, I should say I am, the son of a grocer." He cleared his throat, stared at the painting in front of Helena as if gathering courage. "I grew up in a town smaller than Esperança. In the store and the rooms behind the store where we lived, my parents and older brothers and sisters and I. When I was young..."

"Like Luis," Helena said.

"Younger than Luis," Tomás said, "and not as beautiful. At a time when other boys sit on their fathers' laps and hear stories of great exploits among the men, I sat on my father's lap and watched him use his adding machine. I would sit on his knee while he sat on his stool behind the counter calling out prices for the customers."

Helena could picture the shop—long bars of flecked soap, lengths of tobacco cut from a coil as black and menacing as a jungle snake, wedges of yellow cheese, oats scooped out of a barrel, rope halters, tins of beef, handfuls of nails, chunks of brown sugar, balls of twine, cigarettes and pencils bought one at a time from boxes on the counter. She could see the little boy, looking not so different from the man, light brown hair falling over his earnest forehead, little legs dangling off to one side of his father's legs as he concentrated on his father's fascinating machine.

"There was no cash register, just a lidded wooden box kept under the counter. The money never intrigued me. But the adding machine... I had seen my father pull the cover off to replace the paper roll. It was easy enough to get it off. So, one day, I did it. And took the thing apart, to see who was making it work."

Helena laughed.

"You thought there was a tiny person inside?"

"I did. Funny to remember. And I remember my father's face when he came out from his nap and saw what I had done. He didn't spank me, though, just told me to put his machine back together. Now that I think of it, he might not have known how to do it himself.

"It was the perfect punishment. I sat at the counter on a tall stool brought from our kitchen and worked on that machine for what seemed like days."

No playing in the sun with his brothers, Helena thought. No drawing on scraps of paper at his father's counter, no wandering off in the dark to look at a sky that might have captivated him even then, stars dusting the black like sugar sprinkled on burnt bread. A dreamer child like her own Luis, she was sure, sweet and adored. He must have looked lost in a universe of his own making, peopled with figures outlined in shards of light.

"I probably wasn't there very long, but I thought it was an eternity. Somewhere along the way, I noticed my father was writing down the prices when he called them out for his customers. I couldn't understand why he was doing it the hard way. So, when the next person came up, I just blurted out the total as soon as my father finished reading out the prices. My father looked over at me and I thought I was in trouble again.

"And he asked you how you knew the number, and you couldn't answer him," Helena said.

"As I said, it's a simple story," Tomás said.

"And then?"

"My father's friend said they should test me. He picked up several things off the counter. My father must have called to my mother, because she came from the kitchen and stood behind me with her apron still on."

"And you, the brightest boy, gave them the correct sum," Helena said. She was delighted to see a blush rising from Tomás' collar up to his cheeks. He was quiet.

"Please continue," she said. She looked down at her sketch pad, with its pencil drawing of a small angel that was starting to resemble a little boy in a dusty mercantile. She began looping circles around the tiny face, circles within circles.

"Sr. Homer, the town schoolteacher was brought in to see my little trick. I remember a crowd came with him. Every time my father held up his piece of paper to verify my answer, the people in the store applauded. These people had all known me since I was a baby. Some of them told me later they had never seen anything remarkable in me. Others swore they noticed something about my eyes the first time they looked in the cradle behind the counter," Tomás said, laughing.

"I think I probably just spent too much time on my father's lap listening to sums."

"You're not telling the whole story. I know from your references that you also taught yourself to read at a very young age."

"Well, yes. That trick was discovered the same afternoon, and it almost got me in trouble with Sr. Homer, I think, because I had learned to read without his instruction. But he was a smart man and turned the situation around by announcing to the group in the store that he would give me tutoring and see that I became a teacher."

"And the good Sr. Homer brought you to university."

"He did. He found a scholarship for me and accompanied me to the capital city. And when he returned from his only visit to the capital, the mayor of my little town bestowed the title of Grandmaster on him."

"Was it a great shock coming to my city?"

"More than anyone could have told me. But I couldn't go home. I would have shamed myself and my parents. That kept me there until I found Leonardo."

Helena paused, her pencil hovering over her paper.

"You speak as if he's alive."

"Perhaps he is for me."

"He gave you art."

"Art, anatomy, architecture, the natural and mechanical world. And the stars. Until I read that he studied the heavens, I thought I was the only one who looked at the stars."

And so, Helena thought, he pulls his bed from the corner of his room to rest in the comfort of his window of stars. He draws up the coverlet made for him by another woman and looks out on a night sky, seeing there the pattern for his life.

Chapter 10

✦ ✦ ✦

Helena and Tomás fell into a daily pattern, taking no formal lunch, no afternoon rest, going straight from morning to the art lessons that had become an obsession for Helena.

They drank tea with brown sugar syrup, ate sliced mangoes from a common plate. Tomás cut slabs of bread, hot from the cook's steaming oven, and handed them to Helena as she worked. The boys took their noon meal in the kitchen. Roberto, coming home and finding the dining table covered with drawings and his own meal waiting in the kitchen, gave Helena dark looks for a time and finally asked, "How long will this go on?"

"Please be patient, Roberto. I only want to learn enough to paint a portrait that captures you."

Roberto accepted her answer, tried eating with the boys in the kitchen, then stopped coming home at noon, eating his lunch of cold meat and black bread in the small, windowed office overlooking the factory floor. The boys missed him and questioned the cook, who told them to hush.

◆ ◆ ◆

Helena drew Leonardo's angel again and again, the angle of his bent knees, the turn of his neck as he gazed up at Jesus, the cascade of curls falling away from his translucent face. She copied other Leonardo sketches, drew legs and arms, muscles and sinew, faces and parts of faces.

And she painted—small glimpses of Leonardo's angel, the folds of his blue cloak, tendrils of fine hair, the burnish of his halo. She drew and painted and painted and drew. Tomás guided her, taught her the techniques he knew, gently pointed out excesses that could destroy the pieces.

It was slow, absorbing work. Helena could remember only one other time she had felt like this, the days and months after Luis was born. Then, she could look at his face for hours, trace his perfect features with the tip of her little finger, watch him sleep until she was sure the intensity of her gaze would wake him.

Even so, her all-consuming love for her son had not engaged her heart in exactly the same way. That love was unconditional, complete. This new love was something to be tested against her own limitations, something that would never be wholly satisfied.

She worked as long as Tomás would allow, often asking him for just another hour. There was a fever in her that would not let her go. Tomás sensed it, felt helpless against its heat. He worried she would exhaust herself but longed for the slow morning hours with the boys to hurry, hurry, so he could seat himself again near Helena, surrounded by the dining room's pool of light and watch, through half-closed lids, the woman unfolding under his care.

✦ ✦ ✦

While she worked, Tomás told her stories, about his days at university, about friends and professors there, about Leonardo.

"I first heard of him in an art class. I joined it almost on a whim. As the old women say, God sometimes takes you down paths you can't see for the dust blowing. It was only later that I realized where I had been led. I thought I was just taking a break from my science and math."

In fact, he had been desperate, looking for any antidote to his growing anxiety that university might not be the right place for him. Until he stumbled into his art class and a professor who recognized a fellow traveler, he had been friendless and lonely. His shyness was mistaken for arrogance. His questions, innocently asked in the belief that knowledge would be shared with him gladly, were seen by professors as an affront and by students as an attempt to flatter his teachers. Only the art professor encouraged him.

"The first time my professor mentioned Leonardo, I thought he was speaking of a mythological character. I couldn't imagine a human being that brilliant. I saw that my professor felt the same way. It had never occurred to me that a professor could have a hero, someone he knew was above him.

"It was an exciting time for me. I began to see the world as Leonardo might have seen it," Tomás said. "Understand, I'm not saying I have his eyes. No one will ever see everything he saw. But my view of the world expanded. It became a place of limitless knowledge, infinite beauty. I even thought for a time that I might become a serious artist."

He had taken up the cloak of art, flung it around his shoulders like an ill-fitting coat, proclaimed himself an artist among artists. For the first time since coming to university, he had friends, young men and women who were equally passionate about the creative life.

Women saw him as mysterious, not shy, exotic in his awkwardness. He took up his night walks again, at first alone, then accompanied by one young woman or another. Each listened to his stories of the stars, received his tentative attempts at poetry. Each hoped she would become known as the artist's mistress.

His affairs were fiery but burned out quickly. None of the women stayed in his bed or his memory for long. Only the stars and his painting mattered.

"And so you studied until you became a master artist," Helena said.

"No, Helena," he said quietly. "In the end, I had to admit I would never create anything beautiful, because I did not have the gift. My role would be to teach the truly gifted."

Even now, the memory of that moment pained him, as though his soul had been singed at the edges. It had come to him without warning, a small note from his beloved art professor, asking him to drop by his office. He walked in unaware. His teacher had been kind but blunt. The other professors felt they owed him the truth. His talents were small, would never carry him to the heights he longed for. He was smart, a good student. The university would help him find a teaching position.

He went straight from graduation to a post at a boys' school in the city.

For four years, he endured a private nightmare. By the time they reached age 12 and Tomás' classes in science and math, the boys were used to being bullied by their teachers and other, older students. Most of them had little respect for someone who wanted to give them a gentle world of stars and numbers and art. He became, like his professor before him, a friend to the friendless, a safe harbor for the most timid boys, the dreamers like himself

"And did you find students who were marked by a rare gift?" Helena asked.

You, he wanted to say. You are my masterpiece.

"One child," he said, "so quick to grasp everything, anything. One child out of all those students. Still..."

That boy brought him the attention of the headmaster, who was pleased to find a genius in his school at last. The headmaster's daughter, perhaps with her father's encouragement, also noticed Tomás for the first time.

He courted her for six months or more, knew after a short time that he could marry her, have a job for life, perhaps become headmaster himself one day. He would paint on weekends. He would look at his dimming night sky on infrequent night walks, become known as an old eccentric as his own stars winked out one by one.

One night he woke in a panic. His heart was pounding, his breath ragged.

He was afraid he would die right there. He was afraid he would live a long life and then die in this same bed, or in a nearby room, safe and full of remorse. He loathed his work and many of the boys sitting in his classroom. He did not love the headmaster's daughter. He had never loved any woman. He had no passion to guide him, nothing burning bright in his life. Only his art and his stars mattered, and they had been taken from him.

Down the hall from his room, his students were sleeping. Bully or victim, smart or dull, they all took their measured breaths equally in the night. Tomás heard them breathing as one, heard their breath exhaling over his racing pulse. He forced himself to slow his breathing, to match the long sighs of the sleeping boys.

His fear slid away. He pulled back the covers, sat on his bed in a calm despair.

For the first time, he saw himself clearly. A man adrift. A man whose life had been planned from the days he sat on his father's lap and learned to add sums in his head. That trick—so seemingly harmless—had turned his life forever in a new direction. For good or ill, he was marked, set apart as the boy who would be educated.

He knew without that education he could have ended up running the family store with his brothers. He might have discovered painting on his own, or not. He would have wandered his skies in the night, been laughed at in his small town or called a lunatic. University had made him and university had undone him.

He sat in his small room until dawn pushed at his window. Then he dressed, roused the boys for breakfast and walked to the headmaster's office to request letters of recommendation. He gave no explanation and none was asked.

He received two offers. The first was from another school in a larger southern city, the second from Helena. Tomás did not hesitate. He resigned and, as soon as the school year ended, he left. He did not say good-bye to anyone. He knew he was being cruel. He told himself the headmaster's daughter would forget him. And then, he forgot her.

In the last days at his school, he longed for Esperança, though he had never seen it. He could imagine the dusty village clinging to the edge of the world. He knew it was a place like his home town, a place to find peace. Under the protective and weighty title of teacher, he could pursue any passion—astronomy, art, mathematical puzzles, even architecture or poetry. He could observe whatever small wonders were to be found there. He could free himself from intimations of failure.

When he was refreshed, he would move on to another city, a place of vast museums, observatories with huge telescopes trained on the heavens, cafés full of art students who would admire him and women who would love him.

He saw all this happening. What he did not foresee, at the end of his trip upriver in a canoe full of giggling schoolgirls, was Helena.

"And yet, your brilliant student was not enough to keep you there," she said to him.

"I needed more, Helena. The school, I will admit, was stifling to me. I wanted something to move me again," he said. "I needed to be with the stars."

She thought of her father, sitting in his dusty warehouse amidst his tempting crates or walking through the stalls and shops of the docks. Searching, always searching for the beautiful, the ugly, the sacred and the profane. Wanting to experience everything, no matter the cost.

This was a familiar desire, her father's legacy to her. He had been drawn to a job his parents thought beneath him and his wife found filthy and rough. Helena had been led into that world by her father and then stepped beyond it. Desire had enticed her to Esperança and into the arms of Roberto. It had led her to this moment with Tomás.

"And that is why you came to us," she said. "To see something wondrous—our stars hanging low in this place without light."

She looked across the table at him, and he took in her look. The air was still. The cook paused in her work, the boys were quiet. The brown land stretched out beyond the kitchen door, out from Esperança, out and out to timeless green jungle while Helena and Tomás gazed at each other.

"I wondered what would draw a man away from his art and his books," Helena said, after a time. "Away from his friends and his girls with skirts of light."

"The sky here is immense, Helena. Pure and immense. I could lose myself in your sky."

Chapter 11

+ + +

Helena was tiring. Tomás saw it around her eyes, shadows that would not leave even after a night's rest. He thought of telling her to stop painting but knew he could not. He approached Roberto—perhaps a trip to her city? It was time for her to see canvases, he said, feel brush strokes, study painted eyes and listen to the thoughts behind them.

Roberto gave him a long look that silenced him, then told the boys they were going on a trip to Papa's plantation to see portraits of their dead ancestors and meet their living relatives.

Helena agreed, saying they must leave as soon as possible. Once she had spoken, the wheels of the universe began to turn in a new direction. The cook began planning dishes to be prepared for the boat ride and food to be taken to Roberto's family—hot pepper relishes and mango chutneys spiced with ginger, hearts of palm in vinegar brine, crystallized pineapple, peanut brittle, doces made with the peaches from Helena's tree, coconut cake so light it was legendary on the plantation though the family had tasted it only once, when Roberto and Helena came to visit soon after their wedding.

Carmelinha, who would accompany Helena to the plantation, and the other maids began airing out trunks and clothes—cotton shorts and gauzy white shirts for the boys, lawn shirtwaists for Helena, leather riding breeches for everyone.

A seamstress came in every afternoon for two weeks to cut emerald and amethyst silk bolts from Helena's wedding trousseau into sweeping dinner skirts and make the boys' first pairs of long pants.

Roberto protested a little, not at the expense, but the bother. "The plantation is not a formal place, Helena."

She had the seamstress make an embroidered shirt for him with flowing sleeves and a trim waist and saw him smile.

An additional laundress was hired to take on the extra washing and ironing needed to prepare for the long visit. José glimpsed the new laundress only once, when she came to the front gate of the big house to be handed the first load of clothes tied up in a soiled linen tablecloth.

As she balanced the bundle on her head and turned to go, he thought for one minute that she was his mother. He couldn't be sure but hid the quiet moment in his mind, seeing again and again the woman's dark hair under the ballooning white laundry bundle, her slender brown neck, one flash of a profile and then her back, shoulder blades sharp through the worn cotton dress.

The boys questioned everyone including the cook about the upcoming trip. "How far?" "How many days now?"

"Does the boat go faster than Papa's horse?" and "Is it true they build bonfires bigger than the house and roast pigs over them and dance around them with crazy masks on?" This last was a story from their father, who could not completely hide his own eagerness to be back at the plantation, though the factory would keep him in Esperança most of the time they were gone.

Helena assured the boys it would be a great adventure, that they would get to play with their cousin Sibella and see everything "just the way it used to be." They weren't sure what she meant but whispered the phrase to each other as a talisman against disappointment.

Tomás worked stories about the plantation into his lessons, described growing seasons and harvest for the sugar cane, showed them a drawing of the huge grinding stones powered by animals, run first by slaves, then by their descendants, workers who still lived on the plantation. The great rollers that had poured out liquid sugar and misery in equal doses were now silenced, Tomás told the boys. Cane was sent by barge to sugar factories in the city.

One morning, the lessons were postponed altogether so that Luis and José could go with Tomás to the river to retrieve a mysterious package. The teacher would tell them nothing about the delivery except that it would accompany them to the plantation.

They set out from the house early, with only a little hot milk in their stomachs and the promise of breakfast with Helena once they returned. Tomás pushed open the iron gates that guarded the house, and they stepped into the morning street.

The cool air that greeted them was fragrant with rich coffee, the sweet yeast of rolls baking in an outdoor oven, dust, old dogs and, somewhere still far away, moist river plants. Other boys were already out, chasing a soccer ball around the dirt street. They stopped their game to watch Luis and José walk by with their teacher.

José looked shyly at them. They all seemed familiar to him, these little boys with their ragged shorts, their warm smells, their calls to each other as they kicked the ball, flattened on one side with a slow leak, up and down, up and down the street. The shouts, the sound of bare feet on the leather ball were a memory resonating in his thin chest, as close to him as his own heartbeat.

He had forgotten the everyday world of the street. Except for the monthly walk to church on Sundays that the priest was in Esperança, José hadn't been out to play in the street since that long-ago day he stepped through the iron gates of Helena's house and was scrubbed clean by Carmelinha.

Tomás stopped in front of a small house faced with crumbling plaster and told the boys to wait for him. When he returned to them, he was carrying a deliciously greasy packet tied with twine.

"Breakfast buns," he said and they continued down the street.

At the river, the boys and their teacher sat down on the bank by the water's edge. Tomás unwrapped his package and handed each boy a still-warm bun laced with cinnamon and sugar. Then he told them to pretend they could see deep into the brown water flowing past them.

"The Rio Branco is not just the water you see. Under its moving surface, there are many depths, each with its own secrets. The river is a ribbon of life, bringing us surprises and hiding surprises. The river brought me to your house and brought your mother to Esperança to marry your father. It brings and it takes away—people and goods and life itself. Life here cannot happen without this ribbon of water.

"There is life in the water and under it. Do you see those grasses?"

He pointed upriver. The two boys nodded in unison, both faces serious and intent on the water, both mouths smeared with cinnamon sugar.

"Those grasses go down into the water, down and down to the river bottom and under the rich dirt of the river bottom where they root. Fish swim through the grasses and nibble on them; small snails attach themselves to the grasses; big fish wait there in hiding for the little fishes. The grasses grow up from the river floor, up through the water and into the air, and the river flows over it all, hiding the grasses and the fish and the earth that lies under it. The river is the life blood of everything that lives in it and on it and around it."

José thought of his fisher father, thought of him hauling in nets of struggling fish out of the ribbon of life, fish flailing so hard against the pull of the net that his father came home too tired to do anything but unroll his hammock and lie down.

Tomás told the boys to wash off their faces and hands in the river, to take off their shoes and socks and let the water flow over their feet.

José looked at his feet in the water, watched them change shape, stretch and then shrink as the river rippled around them. He thought of the small fishes swimming in and out of the waving water grasses. He saw the green grasses swaying as if caught in a slow wind. He saw hair waving in the grasses, caught in the grasses, hair waving as a body hung helpless in the heavy grasses, stretching and twisting, mouth opening and closing, letting out no sound, taking in nothing but water.

He stood up in a panic, turned as if to run, and heard a great motor roar as the barge slowly rounded the bend in the river. Tomás was standing beside him, waving his arms.

José saw that his teacher had also taken off his shoes and socks and had rolled his black pants up to his knees. Tomás waded out toward the barge floating calmly in the river and was tossed a large, flat case that he carried high over his head and set carefully on the bank.

He told the boys to hurry up with their shoes. Then he let them help carry the case back through the now hot, still streets of Esperança.

When they reached the house, they took the heavy case into the kitchen, laid it gently on the cook's scrubbed table. The boys watched Tomás undo the two silver clasps at either end of the case and insert a small key from his pocket into the shiny lock.

Then he opened the lid. Luis and José looked inside and saw, fitted into velvet lining like a precious violin, the wood cylinders and glass lenses of their teacher's telescope.

CHAPTER 12

✦ ✦ ✦

HELENA, TOMÁS AND THE BOYS arrived at the plantation dock in the early afternoon and were met by a driver with a horse buggy made of shiny wicker.

A second driver, the biggest, blackest man either of the boys had ever seen, waited with a mule team and wooden wagon to carry the luggage. The boys, excited by the boat trip, climbed in and out of the buggy while the driver and Tomás piled trunks and boxes and baskets of food into the wagon.

Carmelinha, blushing furiously, was pulled onto the wagon seat by the driver, who leaned down from his perch and scooped her up like a great owl swooping down on a mouse. Tomás handed her two birdcages full of twittering and jittery parakeets, presents for the cousins. She propped one cage on each small knee.

As soon as Helena and the boys climbed into the buggy, Luis fell soundly asleep with his head in his mother's lap. She stroked his hair and smiled at Tomás, who was answering the hundredth question from José.

They rode first onto a sparse, brown plain, as flat and dry as the earth of Esperança, then slowly drifted toward waves of brilliant green, fanning out in front of them like the promised land.

"Sugar cane," Helena said and Tomás nodded. It undulated through the moist air, rippled and beckoned. Heat rolled over them, covered them like a smothering quilt.

They rode on and on behind the driver perched high above them, the masthead of their small boat. Their buggy plunged down the dirt road, parting the tall reeds of sugar cane like a miracle.

They passed two men walking shirtless down their road, machetes thrust into leather belts as though pirates strolled these seas. They passed a woman carrying a water jug on her head. In front of her, a small boy danced around a little dog with three legs. They rode into a drowsy sleep, lulled by the rhythmic rocking of their buggy, swaying through the watery trough of air.

Only once did the scene assault them, suddenly revealing a dirty streak of brown against the lush green. Helena roused herself, leaned toward Tomás carefully to keep from waking Luis.

"What are the low buildings?" she asked.

"Workers' houses, I imagine."

"I don't remember them from the last visit."

"When the slaves became free men, they were sent out to build new lives," Tomás said. "Most of them stayed right where they were, took the earth they worked as slaves to make their houses, started a new day going to the same fields they worked the day before as slaves."

The houses, linked by common walls to keep the land free for planting, disappeared in the landscape, swept away by yet another wash of sweet sugar cane.

They rode on. The heavy afternoon pressed down on them like a mother's care, like God's commandment. The birds balanced in their cages on Carmelinha's knees were quiet, stunned into silence by the weight of the heat. José curled against Tomás and slept. Helena placed her white lace handkerchief lightly over Luis' quiet face to shield his sleeping eyes.

They rode endlessly on, until the billows of fresh green cane surged against a second, darker green, the rolling lawn of the big house.

The casa grande rose before them, a vision in the green wilderness, an invitation from God or the devil to enter its cool rooms and lie down forever, forsake the heat and whatever future lay before them. Its deep verandas, running the length and width of the house on both floors, called to them. "Come in, come in and rest."

It stood lonely against the landscape, a fortress against whatever had come before, whatever would follow. Helena knew there were other buildings beyond the big house—the senzala that had housed slaves, granaries and stables for the chained animals that had once pulled the great grinding rollers guided by their chained masters, the ghostly mill and kettle house where the sugar was boiled, even a small, isolated chapel she had glimpsed but never entered on her first visit to the plantation. All this lay beyond the big house. But everything was hidden by the house owned for all time by Roberto's family.

They rode right up to the front steps and waited, as though lost. Then the tall double doors were flung open and Dona Teresa hurried out to greet them.

She looked from Helena to Tomás and back again, then came down the wide front steps with open arms as Luis and José sat up abruptly.

"Helena, of course." Teresa embraced Helena as she stepped down from the buggy.

"You are a woman now, not the child Roberto brought to us eight years ago. We were shocked."

Teresa laughed, then looked again at Tomás.

"The boys' tutor," Helena said. "Sr. Tomás, this is Dona Teresa, Sr. Machado's cousin. She has the plantation now."

"Come in out of this heat. It tried to kill me long ago and failed, but it will kill you and steal your children if you let it. Was the boat trip as long as it used to be? It's too much for my bones. I prefer to stay here on my little piece of ground and boss around the old men."

She laughed again and herded them up the wooden steps and through the tall doors.

"Are you little boys tired? Poor little meninos. You should have a nap and let your mother rest."

She looked down at two small, disappointed faces gazing up at her, leaned down and hugged them both at once, jostling them like little lambs being herded into the safe pen of her large arms. Luis giggled and hugged her back, his arms stretching wide across her middle. José peeked out from the embrace with big eyes.

"You can meet Sibella after naps," Teresa said. "She's your littlest cousin."

She sent the boys off with Carmelinha, then turned to Helena with concern on her face.

"Wouldn't you like to have a rest as well?"

"If I may, I want to see the portraits," Helena said.

⋆ ⋆ ⋆

Long hallways, long, dark hallways, some lined with polished wood cupboards storing linens, vases, porcelain serving ware from the time of kings, silver candelabra black with age, wooden walking sticks, leather hats, straw hats, hammocks, lacquered boxes inlaid with ivory and mother of pearl holding yellowed papers, now tattered along folded edges, proclaiming ownership of land and men.

Narrow Moorish rugs, used to wrap heavy chairs and bedsteads shipped over from the ancestral house three centuries before, carpeted the hallways. Helena and Tomás followed them to room after room of waxed parquet floors and walls painted mauve and rose and yellow.

The walls spoke of hands long forgotten, palms dipped in dyes made with beetle wings and crushed flowers to tint the plaster. Pale palms that ever after carried the stain of the walls, as though they were part of the house itself.

Down the blackest hall, moving almost by touch alone, Helena found a deeply carved door. She pushed it open. It gave with a groan, as though forgotten, revealing a small room painted fading crimson and smelling of old roses. But it gleamed inside with candles freshly lit, votive offerings in red beaded glass lining a narrow, hinged altar pushed against the back wall. The altar, which climbed the wall almost to the smoky ceiling, was the only object in the room.

Helena approached it, made the sign of the cross and saw that the Virgin Mary, despite her holy robes, was sitting on a high shelf in the center panel of the gold-leafed triptych. Her legs hung over the edge of the shelf, her feet bare, as though she had come to the altar in exhaustion, seeking refuge.

In her arms, she held the baby Jesus. But her gaze was directed not at her own child, but downward, to a small painting below her of another perfect baby in a coffin. His eyes, and it was unmistakably a male child, were closed. Each dark eyelash brushed the lower lid like a lost prayer.

Tomás and Helena wandered unbidden and unnoticed through tangles of rooms, living and dead, used or closed up as if patiently waiting for occupants long gone. Nothing was familiar to Helena. No room welcomed her back, as though her first visit, as a bride on the arm of her proud husband, had been a childhood dream.

Somewhere far off, machinery throbbed. There was a sharp shout, dead silence. No one appeared. No one questioned where Helena and Tomás went, what they saw, who they were or why they were there. They traveled alone.

They arrived at last in the dining room, home to most of the portraits, home once to the polished table now standing in Helena's house.

Helena saw her table in this room, saw people she had never known taking their last rest on her table, surrounded by heavy flowers giving off vapors of perfume, flanked by three-foot candles sending smoke and supplications into the ceiling's high beams. She saw the mourning survivors stroking lifeless hands, whispering secrets to ears that could not hear, kissing lips that would never speak.

She saw herself sitting with Tomás at her table hour after hour as they talked of art, sketched, fed each other bread and butter. Saw, for the first time, the sacrifice made to lift the massive table from its true home in this room, wrap it in flannel blankets and send it by barge and wagon to her front gate. Teresa's new dining table was longer, narrower, less ornately carved than Helena's, not as fine.

The room glowed, not with any natural light, for it was an inside room like her own, but with the light of a huge chandelier of painted glass and, it seemed, from the walls themselves. There was a murmuring sound in her ears. Voices, soft from long silences, were speaking to her. The paintings were coaxing her into the room, urging her to come closer to hear their stories.

She stepped further into the room as though blind, guided only by sound. The whispers became a humming, a buzzing drone. The chandelier flickered, the portraits darkened.

Tomás caught her as she fell.

◆　◆　◆

She awoke after dark, confused and worried for Luis until Carmelinha, waiting in a small wicker chair by her bed, ran to fetch Teresa.

Teresa came with hot tea. The teapot with its vining roses reminded Helena of her mother's treasure, the pot she had carried every day as a young girl to the closed shed door where her Gabriel was rising from his clay.

She did as Teresa told her, drank tea from a porcelain cup, sitting up in her bed. Then she asked to see Luis and José.

"They're playing, dear," Teresa said, but sent Carmelinha off to find them. When they came in to say good night, Luis was holding the hand of a little girl with cascading auburn hair.

"Sibella," Teresa said, "come meet your cousin Helena. This is my granddaughter, my angel."

Sibella came forward, Luis in tow, took Helena's hand where it lay on the white linen coverlet and kissed it.

"Meu anjinho," Teresa said again and stroked Sibella's hair.

"Don't be afraid, Luis," Helena said and held out her arms to her son. "I'm fine now."

He hugged her distractedly, his eyes never leaving Sibella. José, just behind him, moved shyly forward to give Helena a hug, burying his face in her neck for one daring moment, letting go only when Teresa said, "Now out, little ones. Your mother needs her rest."

It was then, as the boys and Sibella ran past Teresa, that Helena saw Tomás standing in the doorway. His face was in shadow.

CHAPTER 13

✦ ✦ ✦

THE NEXT AFTERNOON, Helena insisted on getting up, insisted she must see the paintings again.

Teresa brought her sweet tea brewed from a healing plant growing near the kitchen, poured it from the vining pot, made her wear an embroidered satin bed jacket that Teresa herself had worn only after the birth of her first child. It was large on Helena, wrapped around her like the arms of a tender mother.

Helena let Teresa retie the pale blue bow for her, rearrange the pillows yet again. Then she said she should dress soon.

"You're too tired, dear," Teresa said. "You mustn't go too far into the paintings. You'll tempt the gods."

Helena gazed at her husband's cousin calmly, at her kind, wide face, her wisps of graying hair wandering out of the hasty bun, and said, "I did come to see the paintings, Teresa. To see you again, of course. I've missed you more than I knew. And the paintings."

Teresa tried sending Tomás in to reason with her. He approached Helena's bed carefully, sat down in the same wicker chair Carmelinha had used for her vigil the night before, took Helena's white hand in his own hands.

Helena said, "Tomás, please," a smile crossing her face at the sight of him in the tiny chair, his long legs stuck out awkwardly in front of him.

"Men," said Teresa, when Tomás passed her in the hall.

And so Tomás and Helena took the long walk back to the dining room. This time, the walls were quiet, the paintings silent. Only the eyes told Helena they were still with her, marking her presence among them.

She moved through them slowly, touching them, feeling thick ridges of ancient oil on rough canvas, thin washes over smooth wood. Small flecks of paint clung to her fingertips. She fought the urge to lick her fingers.

Tomás stood back, saying nothing, watching her progress through the sometimes overpowering, sometimes awkward paintings. Until she came to one small portrait with a frame of gilt too large for the delicate face looking out at them as through a distant window.

Helena did not touch the painting, as if to do so would be to touch living flesh. The girl looked ready to fly away at any sudden movement. Resolute but fragile, her young face still full of color and promise, but washed over with some threat that left smudges under her eyes.

She looked like Helena.

Helena stood quietly in front of the girl, whose eyes pleaded with her.

"It is the best in the room, in the house from what I've seen," Tomás said. "The only one worthy of your time. You must study this one portrait, Helena. But we'll need to be careful. There is something dangerous about her."

"She's in pain," Helena said.

They leaned into the frame, heads bent together much as they had leaned together over Helena's table, sharing words and bread and butter and long silences, much as they had come together in moonless dreams, long bodies twisting like grasses of the river, like sweet sugar cane in the slow moments before Helena awoke in her own bed.

She moved in front of Tomás, her skirt brushing his legs. Looking deeply into the girl's face, Helena saw something fierce burning quietly behind the shadowed eyes, saw the small, sharp teeth behind closed lips. She stepped back into Tomás' body, felt his breath in her hair as the painting tried to pull them in.

"I see you've found Célia."

Teresa was coming up noisily behind them, between them.

"She's our family's only beauty—or was until you came along, Helena. She's a good lesson for our little girls, a good reason to be plain. That's what I always told myself when I cared about those things. The world doesn't spare the beautiful ones, especially if they bring the wrath of the angels down on themselves."

Teresa stopped to take a breath.

"Goodness, I do rattle on. I came to tell you supper's ready. There are meats for everyone else and a good broth for you, Helena. It's laid out in the kitchen. Through here, dear."

She led Helena away from Tomás, away from the seductive painting, which Helena heard hiss faintly as she moved beyond its power.

✦ ✦ ✦

Helena woke in her dark bedroom to drumming and did not know she was awake. She felt the pulsing beat more than hearing it, as if her heart and the walls of her room were one. The house was a lover, leaning over her, breathing with her, urging her out of her bed to follow, follow.

Helena resisted, lay quiet as death and heard the drumming stop, then resume. She found the center of the sound, pursued it in her mind, pushed open the deeply carved door, entered the room of old roses, votive candles guttering, close smell of decaying flowers, entered and saw only black.

She put her hands over her ears. Willed her heart to slow, until it did not match the drumming. And slept again.

CHAPTER 14

+ + +

HELENA OPENED HER BOX OF PAINTS and inhaled, once again, the deep odors of color. She had not seen the silver tubes for a long time. The preparations for the plantation visit had taken more from her days and weeks than she had realized.

Seated at her small easel in front of the painting, Helena settled into Célia's presence with anticipation. This girl would be her most challenging work. But she felt she understood the face looking out at her, saw the child behind the young woman's eyes and sensed an intelligence that she hoped she could paint into her portrait.

As soon as Helena picked up her charcoal to make the first line on her canvas, a gray light descended. She glanced over her shoulder at the chandelier, thinking it had dimmed. It was still burning but, like everything else in the room, seemed dampened, mottled. The light was coming from the painting itself. Célia's face, so brilliant and compelling when Helena first looked at her, was veiled. The girl seemed to have second thoughts about Helena's portrait.

Helena struggled alone with her sketching, hesitating over each stroke. She stopped when Tomás came in.

"Do you want to review some of your lessons?" he asked when he saw her face.

Helena shook her head.

"Perhaps you should begin with another portrait? Something simpler."

"No, Tomás. I need to work with this painting," she said. She did not tell him what she knew, that if she did not take up the challenge the girl presented, she would not paint again. She would fail in her promise to paint Roberto with his sons, fail in her secret wish to offer God the best of his work—her beautiful son.

Each noon, the family entered the dining room and found Helena's easel covered with a cloth. All questions were met with a polite smile and silence. Helena would not show anyone, not even Tomás, the shape of paints on her canvas.

Each afternoon, after the dishes had been cleared and the household rested, Helena sent Tomás away and stood alone in front of her easel. She tried to remember his words, the lessons he had given her while she painted Leonardo's beautiful angel, the encouragement and praise he offered. But Célia would not yield to her. For the first time since she had unwrapped the fragrant box from Os Olhos de Michelangelo in her kitchen, Helena questioned herself.

Her brush was heavy. Her fingers could not hold it. Each hour, it seemed, the painting changed. The girl's glance would slide sideways in an almost mocking look, retreat from Helena, go deep where she could not follow.

Colors shifted, grew pale or dense. The shape of the girl's mouth altered subtly, looking soft one minute, hard and bitter the next.

Each time Helena bent to her paints, she could feel Célia's contemptuous eyes on her, mocking her.

✦ ✦ ✦

After many days, Tomás announced at lunch that Helena needed a room with better light for her painting. Before dessert had been served, he took Célia from the wall and disappeared. When he returned, he told Helena to bring her canvas and follow him. The room he led her to was her own bedroom.

"This window," he said, "is small but the light is good. Look at Célia."

He held the painting up to the window. Helena saw the girl relax in the warm afternoon light. The small face glowed. Her eyes looked directly at Helena for the first time since the work had begun. A smile played around her mouth.

"She's beautiful again."

"She is. You will be able to paint her here. She will teach you all you need to know."

Helena placed her canvas on its easel and stepped back to let Tomás see her work. For one moment, he thought that the canvas was blank. It was not. Subtle layers of color, residue of Helena's oils, stained the cloth. Each day, Helena was repainting Célia's face. Each day, she was scraping off that day's work, erasing everything she had accomplished.

No face was yet apparent, but the shifting layers, laid over the ghosts of the previous day's work, gave the impression of a strong presence. When the final colors were spread on the canvas, the girl would live. The breath, the life force, was already there. Helena was creating a painting that began not with bones and muscle, but with the very soul of the girl.

Tomás had read about master artists who scraped off each day's painting, day after day, sometimes for months, until they had learned everything they needed to create a particular painting. But he had never seen anyone do it, not his professors, certainly not his students. Helena had come to the idea by her own instincts.

He saw that, once again, she was reaching beyond anything he could give her. He marveled that she didn't recognize her gift, still relied on him for guidance. He knew he must relinquish the role of teacher, let her know that she was teaching herself. And he would. Soon, he told himself. Very soon.

◆ ◆ ◆

The family settled into familiar days. Afternoons, the boys let Sibella lead them to forgotten rooms in the house, abandoned slave quarters, hideaways in the cane fields while their mother and teacher closed the door and painted.

Mornings, Helena and Tomás took long walks with the children down rambling dirt roads that crossed the plantation like an ancient, unwritten history. Tomás gave each of the boys and Sibella a sketch pad and set of colored pencils and took them into the fields to capture the birds and plants on paper. Helena made herself useful in Teresa's big kitchen, baking the cakes and custards her own cook had taught her, happy in the easy companionship of her husband's cousin.

Teresa talked about her life as a young mother to four boys, now all grown and gone.

"Those were the good days on the plantation," she said. "Men were plentiful, and women and children filled the big house. Now it's just me and my little angel rattling around in this big place, trying to keep the gods happy and the workers from starving. It's good to have you here. I haven't heard Sibella giggling like this since her daddy's last visit."

Teresa thought the time would come to ask Helena about the painting lessons in her bedroom. The time did not come, and Teresa told herself she was just being a suspicious old woman.

CHAPTER 15

✦ ✦ ✦

"IT'S MORNING, MAMA." Helena felt small hands on her face, opened her eyes and looked into the eyes of her son.

"Teresa has promised us an excursion." Luis looked so serious, as though Helena might refuse to get up, as if she could refuse him anything.

"An excursion?" she smiled at him. "What do you think an excursion is?"

"I don't know, but she says it will be fun and full of fresh air. I believe her."

He skipped away from Helena's bed, ran to the door, shouted, "She's coming soon," into the hall, ran back to Helena.

"You are, aren't you?"

"Yes, my darling Luis, if you say so. Let's see what sort of excursion Teresa has planned for us."

Breakfast was only coffee for Helena. The children had already eaten; the horses were saddled and waiting.

"It's just a short trip out to the springs," Teresa told Helena after the boys ran out into the courtyard to meet

99

their ponies. "But I thought it would be an adventure for the meninos."

"You're too good to us," Helena said, affectionately. "You'll spoil us so we'll never want to leave. Will we, Tomás?"

"Never," Tomás said.

Helena stepped through the tall, glass-paned kitchen doors into the courtyard. The boys were already on their ponies, Luis looking a little apprehensive, as though he hadn't realized he would be riding a horse he didn't know.

They ambled out through tall, razor-edged cane, looking deceptively soft in the hazy morning air. Once past the high canes and into fields of short, new stalks, the trail widened and they rode three abreast—Tomás in front with the boys, Sibella riding with her grandmother and Helena. Antonio, Teresa's foreman, brought up the rear on his own squat horse, which was burdened with rugs and a large basket.

Tomás began to teach the boys a song about a brave bandido who roamed the countryside.

"Oh, he robbed from the rich and gave to the poor," Tomás sang in a strong baritone. Helena was startled. In her dreams, his songs were in a higher voice. She realized she had never heard his true singing voice.

"Oh, he robbed from the rich and gave to the poor," two warbling voices chimed in.

Sibella looked at her grandmother.

"Well, go on then," Teresa said, and Sibella gave her pony a little tap with her riding stick to urge him closer to Tomás and the boys.

"And if you're good, he knocks on your door."

Teresa snorted.

"If you've been forsaken by God, more like it. That man was no savior. He murdered good people."

"Teresa," Helena said, amused.

"He did. Cut off my uncle's ear because he refused to give him gold. Mother of God, there was no gold in the house. It was everything the family could do to keep the place going and feed the workers. Gold! My uncle trotted out that missing ear story every chance he got. By the time he was an old man, he was fighting off an army to save the plantation."

"Oh, he rode into town a solitary man," Tomás sang and his little chorus answered him.

"Maria was with him when he rode out again."

"Oh, pretty Maria was the fairest in the land..."

The voices drifted back to Helena as the children and their teacher moved further down the trail. The crops had given out to bare earth, a soil so rich Helena could smell its yeastiness. It was the scent her husband carried to her bed after his days at the plantation.

She saw herself taking off heavy riding boots, rooting toes into black dirt, stretching out branch arms, thin fingers turning green at the tips, sprouting profuse leaves. There was nourishment here, something that would not blow away in a strong wind.

For the first time, Helena wondered at Roberto's father, a man dead before she married his son, wondered at his decision to turn his back on the plantation, raise Roberto away from family, on cracked earth that yielded only dust and sadness and cement.

Now she understood why her husband must leave her from time to time. Esperança was his work, his house, the passion and solace of his marriage. Esperança was his childhood. But this land still held his heart.

Helena tilted her leather hat back on her head, let the sun fall on her face. The sunlight seemed diffused, milder than the sere sun of Esperança. Her skin warmed, remembering the heated, wet air of her own childhood. She felt a rush of longing to see her own father again. Her good father, who sent out messages full of news about the crates, with their perfume of foreign hands and breath still clinging to them as they arrived in his dusty warehouse. Her father, who asked always, almost timidly, at the end of every letter, "And you? Are you well, Helena? Are you happy?"

Her mother never wrote, as if Helena had stepped off the edge of the earth when she married Roberto.

◆　◆　◆

The horses trudged up a short rise, and Teresa called to her granddaughter, "Sibella, you lead them. You know the way, meu anjinho."

With little Sibella guiding them, the four horses worked their way through an outcropping of rocks standing like low sentinels against the horizon, then dropped slowly out of sight, as if following a small angel into the earth itself.

Helena could hear Tomás still singing, his voice staccato to the rising sound of rushing water.

"Oh, he rode through the land with the devil on his back," and the children chirping an excited response, "Oh, he rode through the land with the devil on his back. And once he started he never looked back."

"The same could be said for your good teacher's riding," Teresa said to Helena.

"I have to admit he doesn't sit well," Helena said, gazing fondly at the tall figure disappearing into the earth. "But he wasn't raised to it like all of you were."

"We always said Roberto was born into a saddle," Teresa said, "even though his mother was a city girl and his father hated horses. Roberto was always out in the stables when he came here. First thing, off to see the horses, like he had stories to tell them. Even when he was little and sickly. Even when he got older.

"All the girls longed to hear his secrets, but he just spent his days riding through the fields as if he owned the place. We'd have been better off if he had. I loved my husband, God rest his soul, but his mind was always somewhere else, making poetry or mischief. And my brothers were no better. Well, they were better. Helped me keep everything going during the bad times, they did, but still...Roberto and I would have made something of this place. You know that."

"I've never thought of it, Teresa."

"Just look at what he did with the factory. Well, of course, it was already his before he captured you. But I tell you, it was a pitiful thing in his father's day. He didn't know how to work people the way Roberto does."

They reached the rock soldiers, standing guard over the rent in the earth's flat face. Teresa climbed off her horse to lead it down the boulders. Helena followed her on horseback, taking in the scene spread out before her.

Fresh water, pouring from an underground spring high on the opposite side of the cut, rushed over stones and fell into a clear pool. Mist rose up the boulders, watering vines clinging to the stones, ferns sprouting from fissures in the rock. A plant Helena had never seen before—dark, shiny leaves with bursts of small white flowers—grew in the rocks closest to the falls, fed by the splashing water. Its flowers gave off a scent that wafted over her.

A stream led out of the pool, ran for a ways down the cut, then disappeared into the thirsty earth. The spring had created the cut, the cut had created the pool. The clear water had nourished the earth and bestowed an abundance of green life. And then, as if taking back its fruits, the earth swallowed up what it had revealed, gave no further hint of the water flowing under its brown skin.

The boys and Sibella, stripped bare, were already splashing in the pool. Tomás, shirt sleeves shoved above his elbows and pants rolled in a futile attempt to stay dry, was in water up to his thighs. José was resting belly down on his teacher's upturned palms. Tomás was urging him to "kick harder."

José kicked furiously, while Sibella circled them lazily. Luis, in shallow water, jumped up and down like a frenzied cherub, shouting "Me next, me next."

Helena saw that her son was already brown from his days in the plantation sun. Only his round belly and bottom, perfect except for the birthmark shaped like a small, dark crown, were still white.

Tomás guided José, still kicking, safely to shallow water, then picked up Luis, who shrieked with happiness, and carried him out to deeper water.

Helena swung off her horse, removed his saddle, let him walk to the water's edge to drink with the other horses. Teresa had already spread a rug where the graveled shore was shaded by the rocks above it. Helena sat beside her, pulled off her leather hat and long boots.

"This is heaven."

"It's been here for all time," Teresa said. "When I was a child, there were saints perched on a ledge behind the waterfall. I thought they were water sprites that lived in the rocks. I don't know when they disappeared. Sometime in the days I was raising children they must have tumbled into the pool. Like my lost years."

She laughed.

"It's such a short ride, dear. I look there at the boys and Sibella and see myself with my brothers and cousins. We were as fresh as they are. Roberto learned to swim here, you know, not in that smelly river you call home."

"He never speaks of that time," Helena said. "Was he as sweet as Luis?"

"Tougher," Teresa said. "A little José. You were right to give Luis a brother. He would have been too timid without him."

Chapter 16

✦ ✦ ✦

Teresa spread a narrow, striped rug next to Helena and began taking food from the large picnic basket. Helena lifted heavy lids from brown clay pots, smelling each dish in turn—grilled chicken, manioc flour fried in butter with onion, parsley and dried shrimp, a rice salad, hearts of palm in oil and vinegar, black beans cooked with bacon and garlic.

She dipped her finger into the thick black bean sauce, sucked it, tore off a chunk of bread, pulled out the center, filled the hole with white, crumbly cheese.

Teresa watched Helena take a large bite of the fresh bread and cheese.

"You have an appetite," she said. "Good. You can be a painter without starving to death, you know."

Helena laughed.

"I do feel hungrier out here."

She leaned across the rug to peer into Teresa's basket.

"What other treats have you hidden in there?"

"Never mind," Teresa said, closing the lid of the basket. "You can wait just like the children."

She cupped her hands to her mouth and shouted over the splashing and high-pitched squeals from the pool.

"Come get your towels and dry off."

"There'll be no wet, naked children at my table," she said to Helena, "even if it is only a rug."

Tomás herded the children up to the rug, handed them towels, sat down in the sun to let his pant legs dry out.

"The boys will be swimming in no time," he said to Teresa, "just like your water baby."

"That one," Teresa said. "I didn't see her arrive, but I think she came out paddling."

The children, sitting cross-legged in shorts and nothing else, ate like small, hungry animals. Fingers greasy with chicken, cheeks shiny with nectar from the plump mangoes Teresa pulled from her basket and mouths sticky from crunchy coconut macaroons, they ended their feast gnawing on chunks of raw sugar cane.

Teresa poured cups of hot tea for Helena and Tomás— "cold drinks will curdle your food in this heat"—and sent the children off to watch Antonio expertly hack slices out of three coconuts with his machete, exposing the milk inside for them to drink.

Helena leaned back into the warm boulders sheltering her shaded rug, chewed on a piece of sugar cane left by one of the children, drank deeply from her hot tea. The air simmered, heat and water vapor mixing in a thick brew.

Sibella, playing the daring Maria, pranced in and out of the water's edge with the boys close behind her. Their shouts echoed off the boulders, a bright clanging of bells and cymbals. The wet air curled around Helena, caressed her.

She put down her white tea cup, slid down on the rug and fell sound asleep. She slept without dreaming, as though innocent and alone, and heard no sound until she was jerked awake by screams.

She was on her feet and running, knowing it was Luis. Where was he, where was he? Tomás was in the water, deeper, swimming hard toward the little body flailing beyond his reach.

Helena was at the pool's edge before she realized the screams were coming not from the water, but from Luis, standing on the shore. José, now held up by Tomás in deep water, now tucked under one arm as Tomás swam back to Helena, had not uttered a sound.

Tomás and José reached shallow water just as Helena ran to Luis. For one confused moment, they huddled, Tomás and Helena both trying to embrace both boys. Tomás set José on his feet, bent down on one knee to look into his face, pushed his wet hair out of his eyes, held him by the shoulders until the little boy stopped coughing and shaking.

Helena stood in the water, Luis clinging to her, his face buried in her thigh, crying.

"Luis, darling, José is all right. He's all right now." She stroked her small son's head, then, seeing he was still crying, picked him up in her arms and rocked him.

"Stop now, hush. It's all right."

José looked up at his brother with bewilderment. "I'm all right now, see?"

Luis looked down at José. Helena lowered him back to the shallow water.

"He's fine now. He just forgot to go out with Tomás."

"Are you ready to go back?" Tomás said to José.

José nodded his head.

"Good boy."

"Tomás, are you sure?" Helena asked.

"He should."

Helena watched Tomás, soaked from his frantic swim, carry the little naked boy in his arms out to deeper water, lower him carefully into the pool, then raise him and lower him over and over again as if baptizing him.

Helena and Teresa walked back to the rug. Luis refused to let go of Helena's hand, sat when she sat, then crawled into her lap. Sibella, forgotten in the turmoil, walked over to Luis and began patting his arm.

"It's okay, now, it's okay," she said.

Luis didn't move.

After a while, Sibella gave up, waded back into water up to her waist and swam out to Tomás and José.

"See, Luis? You can swim like that," Teresa said.

"No," said Luis.

Tomás, holding José under his belly, guided him back into shallow water, then walked over to Helena.

"Your turn, big boy," he said to Luis.

"No," said Luis.

"You mustn't be afraid, child," Teresa said.

Luis looked at his mother. She nodded. He stood up bravely, took Tomás' hand, walked to the water's edge where José was waiting for him.

"Strange," Teresa said.

"He's just a baby, Teresa," Helena said.

"I mean the birthmarks."

She nodded toward the two boys, facing the water side by side. José had his hand on Luis' arm, seemed to be encouraging him to go into the water. Unlike Luis, he was brown all over. But the dark crown birthmark, a duplicate of Luis', was still visible.

"They were meant to be together," Teresa said.

Her words were cut off as Luis shrieked, ran away from Tomás, back to Helena and hid his face in her lap.

"Leave him be," Helena said when Tomás walked back to her. "He can try later."

✦　✦　✦

They rode home in the blue light of early evening, Tomás pointing out the brightest stars to the children. Soon José and Sibella were singing their silly bandido song again. But Luis, riding with his mother, his pony tied behind Antonio's horse, did not join in.

"Oh, he rode through the land with the devil on his back," the children sang.

Helena, arms wrapped around her son, his little head under her chin, heard him say, "Next time, I won't be afraid."

She hugged him closer.

"Next time, we'll swim in my ocean," she said. "We'll ride the waves together and you won't be afraid at all."

CHAPTER 17

✦ ✦ ✦

ROBERTO WAS WAITING in the courtyard when they rode in.

"Roberto," Teresa said with delight. She swung heavily off her horse, gave her cousin an affectionate hug, then stepped back to look at him.

"You're gray—too much of that cement factory. A few days in the fresh air will do you good."

"I've already been out, Teresa," Roberto said, smiling.

"Surveying our land, were you? Well, tell me what you think. After you say hello to your wife."

Helena walked to her husband, feeling somehow shy. He looked different out here—taller, perhaps, and younger. He bent to kiss her cheek and she smelled fresh earth. She knew he had been crouching beside new, green shoots, crumbling the soil between his fingers for the pleasure of it.

The boys stood together quietly behind their mother, waiting for their father to notice them. Sibella flew past her cousins and hugged Roberto around the knees. He lifted her up and kissed her on the forehead.

"Sweet Sibella," he said, putting her down, then looked at his boys. "You'll have to get into a bath for your mother. Then I want to hear about your ride."

✦ ✦ ✦

After their soup and bread, Helena tucked in the children and heard their prayers. Sibella, in her corner bedroom, demanded the first turn with Helena "because I'm the girl and because I say so." José prayed every prayer he knew, to keep Helena by his bed as long as possible. But she sat with Luis the longest, rubbing his small back until he finally settled into sleep.

When she returned to the kitchen, her husband and his cousin were talking crops over glasses of whiskey.

"You were a long time tonight," Teresa said.

"The children were still excited after today's excursion," Helena said.

"I've planned a little excursion myself for the boys tomorrow," Roberto said, tilting his chair back on two legs. "The sugar house."

"Roberto," Teresa said. "That place is a menace. It should be torn down. I know, I know," she said, waving away his protests. "You would hate that."

"This man," she said to Helena, "would like to see the clock turned back. He's a romantic at heart."

Roberto laughed. "We'd better say good night before you tell more lies about me."

He stood and Helena stood with him, following him to the end of the kitchen and a door she had never opened.

"The back stairs," he said, when she looked at him questioningly. "Home to servants and small boys hiding in the dark."

He smiled down at her and guided her into the gloom of the narrow stairs.

The strong smell of oil assailed them at the door to Helena's room. Roberto stopped for a moment, his eyes adjusting to the dark, then strode to the corner where Célia was hanging.

"What's she doing here?"

"I'm painting her, or trying to."

"I don't want her here."

"Roberto, this is the way Tomás teaches."

"Find another way, Helena."

Helena drew her husband away from the painting in its dark corner, began unbuttoning his shirt as he sat down on the edge of her bed. He let her take off his shirt, watched her run cool water in the small basin by the wardrobe, ring out a cloth.

She went to him, pressed the cool cloth against his forehead, as though soothing a small child, then drew it over his face, down his neck, across his chest. He pulled her into the wedge of his spread legs, rested his forehead on her stomach as she gently washed the back of his neck. Then he stood up into her arms and began undoing the small buttons down the back of her blouse.

◆ ◆ ◆

Helena woke to vibrating air. Echoes of the drums played painfully in her chest. The sound rose, stretched skins keening. The drums did not call to her, they did not play for her. They were lost in their own rhythm and did not want or need her.

Her mind moved along the waves of sound, found the carved door, shrank back, back. Until the waves receded and she fell again into exhausted sleep.

◆ ◆ ◆

It was Roberto who was waiting at the table when Carmelinha led the boys and Sibella into the kitchen for their breakfast.

The boys bumped close in the doorway, not used to seeing their father alone at the breakfast table. Mornings were with Helena who woke them herself with kisses and songs, led them sleepy and warm to their breakfast porridge.

Roberto sat at the far end of the long battered table, cradling a mug of coffee and milk. He raised his head, looked at his boys still in the doorway.

"Come eat," he said, impatiently. "I have something to show you."

The boys and Sibella drank their hot cocoa quickly, never taking their eyes off Roberto. When they were finished, he led them all outside, mouths unwiped, and across a field to the sugar house.

In Roberto's mind, it was always night in the sugar house. The rest of the plantation was daylight, sun and fresh rain, translucent green light slanting off the rows of new cane.

But the sugar house, the place he was taking his boys to see, was the night of his childhood. He was a small boy again, standing in the dark by a fire roaring out of an open hole. It cracked and threw sparks thrillingly close to the cords of wood stacked nearby. Someone was holding his hand, telling him to lean in close, feel the flames that were cooking the sugar.

He wanted to. He didn't want to. He was afraid he would catch on fire like the men feeding the unholy fires, stirring the boiling cauldrons of molten sugar. They moved with dark shadows attached to their feet, moved heavily as though the shadows were weighing them down, holding their feet, sitting on their shoulders. Flames licked at their hands, flickered off their sweat-glazed faces and chests.

And someone was holding him high over the boiling sugar in the big pot. Holding him up and telling him, "That's gold, boy. Don't ever forget it."

"This was a magnificent place," he said to the boys, leading them through the gloom of the boiling room to the row of fire holes.

"These furnaces are silent now. But this place roared like the flames of Hell when these furnaces were fed wood. They burned all night, night after night, until all the cane was in. Cut in the day, just like we do it now. Cooked at night after it had been crushed in the mill. Everything had to be done fast, the right temperature, the right fire, taken off only and exactly when it was done. One man could ruin a whole night's work if he was lazy. The foremen had to keep them all moving, moving, threaten them, do whatever it took. I wish you could have seen it."

He stopped, stared into the black, empty fire holes.

"I want to show you the mill."

He led them back into sudden day. They stumbled and rubbed their eyes, shocked to return to the good, sunlit world they knew. Then they walked into the evening of the mill house.

"Come see the grinding stones."

Sibella looked around with boredom, but the two boys hung behind their father, not sure what was ahead. The massive upright rollers, covered with dust, sat silent and menacing.

Roberto went up to them, stared at them as if imagining a stalk of cane being pulled into their pressing weight, bleeding its sugar into the trough below.

"The rollers were turned by oxen, like we have in the fields now to pull the carts full of cane. Did you see the carts in the yard?"

The boys nodded.

"They don't work now because it's the rainy season," Sibella said.

"Smart girl," Roberto said and she beamed.

"In the old days, when your papa was just a boy, this place was alive. Ox boys no bigger than you two rode the ox teams to keep the rollers turning smoothly. The men cut the cane with their machetes, just like they do now, hauled it in because they were stronger. The women fed the cane into the rollers like they were threading giant needles.

"My grandfather brought me here when I was much younger than you, and told me about his days. The plantation had the best cane and the strongest slaves. Everything a man needed was right here—crops for the table and beef raised on our poor land in Esperança. It was a beautiful place in those days."

He put his hand on the silent stones as if reassuring himself they were still real, all was still possible. José reached out a small hand, laid it flat against a stone in imitation of Roberto.

"Look out," Roberto teased. "It might bite."

José jerked back his hand, then looked sheepish when Roberto grinned at him. But Luis said, "They bite?" in a tremulous voice and Sibella giggled.

"I saw a woman get her arm caught in these rollers," his father said. "We were using horses then to turn the mill. Terrible thing. They're not beasts like the oxen. When her hand went in, she started screaming. That panicked the horses and they ran. In the end, we had to cut her arm off to save her and the rollers."

"Did you do it?" Sibella asked, finally impressed by this place she had grown up with and ignored.

"No, sweet Sibella. I was just a child. But I saw it. I didn't flinch and I didn't cry."

"Luis cried yesterday and wouldn't go swimming," Sibella said.

Luis gave her a miserable look. Roberto gazed at his son. "I don't want any crybabies here," he said.

Chapter 18

+ + +

AFTER ROBERTO LEFT, the rains set in. Helena expected the gusting sheets of water that fell on Esperança. The showers falling on the big house were different, constant and mild. The house settled down, rested in the cool water bathing it after the long summer of heat. The boys, for the first time since their arrival at the plantation, sat quiet and lethargic, listening to Tomás' morning lessons. Raindrops splashed on the fields and drummed softly on the tile roof, playing a distant song two stories over their heads.

The rains continued for days. The house began creaking in odd places and at odd times. Moans and low groans were occasionally heard from rooms never used. Walls in one upstairs room wept. Damp shadows in the shape of a hand and a large bird appeared on the ceiling of a second.

"This house is an old woman, like me," Teresa said, and sent two of her men out on the slick roof to find the source of the weeping.

On the fourth day, the family abandoned the dining room for meals in the kitchen where the back wall of windows let in some light. The air outside was as heavy as old silver. The noon meal stretched out endlessly as the adults drank hot tea with brown sugar and the children took cup after cup of sweet fruit juices or cocoa. Teresa told stories from her childhood on the plantation, the days when everything was bigger, brighter, the bandits more fierce than the legends they left, the sun more brilliant, the rains endless and devastating.

"One year the storms were so bad the birds began falling out of the sky. They drowned flying and drowned on the limbs where they had taken shelter. But that wasn't the worst God had for us. The next year, the rains came early, before we harvested the last crop of cane. The oxen were dropping in the fields trying to pull the loaded wagons through a sea of mud. We all ended up out in the fields, children and housemaids too, pushing through mud up to our knees, wet to the bone."

The boys listened wide-eyed, then ran to Sibella's room to play disaster in the fields.

The rains continued, and the children begged over and over to go out and were told again and again they would suffer illness and worse. They turned restless, then cranky. Mornings, Helena tried to amuse them with silly games and stories from her own childhood. Tomás sat beside her, mute without his lessons.

Luis woke from a nap with the sniffles and was quarantined in his bed. No playmates were allowed, but Helena sat with him morning to dark, coaxing him to drink medicinal teas sweetened with honey and reading Sibella's entire shelf of fairy tale books to him. Sibella and José sat stubborn and morose in the hallway outside Luis' room, feeling more banished than he did.

The third afternoon, Helena left for yet another pot of pungent tea and returned to find two suspicious bumps under Luis' covers and her patient giggling. Luis was declared well, and the three reunited children played happily for several hours before another argument broke out and they were all sent to bed.

◆ ◆ ◆

Helena continued to sit patiently in front of her canvas, working each day on the curve of Célia's cheek or a streak of auburn glinting in her hair. Each evening, she pulled out the small knife wiped clean from the night before and scraped away her day's work.

Tomás continued to work near her, sketching his own versions of Célia on page after page of paper. From time to time, he sat by Helena, watching her work, inhaling the scent of her hair, memorizing the shape of her right hand curved around the brush, learning by heart every line in her knuckles, the shape of each nail, until he could feel her hand's weight in his, could imagine precisely the touch of skin to skin, turning her palm up and raising it to his lips.

"Remember you are painting from the bones out," Tomás said, on yet another drizzling afternoon. Dishes from the noon meal clattered in the kitchen. The children banged hallway cupboard doors outside Helena's bedroom in a noisy game of hide-and-seek.

"Look to the structure first, the anatomy. She is made of bones framed by muscle, sinew, skin."

"She is beyond anatomy, Tomás. She is passion."

"Look to the light, then. Ignore what she is saying to you for the moment. See her as pure light and shadow. Not a beauty, not even a young girl. Just areas of shadow and light."

In the hall, the children's shouts suddenly erupted into a quarrel.

"You peeked."

"I didn't."

"You did."

"I found you."

"You peeked."

Tomás rose from his chair beside Helena, went into the hall.

"You children must keep still now. Be good and as soon as the rain stops, I'll take you for a nighttime excursion."

"Will we go hunting?" Helena heard Sibella ask.

Tomás laughed.

"Yes, but for animals in the sky."

He would say no more.

⚜ ⚜ ⚜

No one thought the rain would stop. Even Teresa took to cursing the heavens, although she carefully left God and her favorite saints out of the litany.

And then, a day of sunlight, as though God stepped back from the world to let it breathe. When Helena walked into the kitchen, the boys and Sibella were already outside with Tomás, testing the steaming ground just beyond the courtyard's brick patio, twittering and silly as small birds just released from their cages.

José noticed first that Helena was seated at the kitchen table, watching them through the wall of windows. But he did nothing until Luis looked up from the square patch of earth he was studying, and said, "Mama." All three children ran into the kitchen, followed by a smiling Tomás.

"It's today, Mama," Luis said.

"I know that it's today, Luis," Helena said, laughing.

"I mean today's the day we go hunting in the sky."

Helena looked at Tomás, who shook his head.

"Not today, Luis. But possibly tomorrow. When the ground is dry enough. I want to show the children the night sky."

"Through his telescope," Luis said, his voice full of wonder. "Remember when we got the telescope, Mama? We walked to the river, and Sr. Tomás rolled up his pants and went into the river to get it."

José remembered the river. He remembered a small, white hand, reaching out under the river, as though the shining surface of water were the untouchable sky, beyond all hope. A small hand waving in a watery breeze. Fluttering like one of his mother's just-laundered handkerchiefs lifting lazily from the grass where she had spread it flat to dry. His mother, whose face, voice, smell, touch were fading from his mind as though she were floating away on a receding river tide.

"Why must the ground be dry?" Helena asked Tomás.

"Because we're making an excursion, Mama," Luis said. "With blankets and ponchos, so we can watch the stars all night."

"Or until we get cold or missing our beds," Tomás said to Helena with a smile. "You should plan to come too. The sky will be full of surprises."

✦ ✦ ✦

The sun held through the next few days, a miracle of warmth and light after the rain. The boys and Sibella ran to the back courtyard over and over, squatting on haunches to touch the ground, willing the earth to stay dry, the good weather to hold.

Tomás told the children to "start scouting a route for our excursion to high ground." Teresa pulled worn blankets from cupboards, rolled and tied them expertly with leather thongs.

"Cattle drives," she said to Helena. "My bedroll was always the softest, and I did get teased the hardest for it. I wish to God I could still sleep out on the ground. These old bones..."

Still, she hesitated before agreeing to let Sibella go with the boys, then said, "Why not? She has to be a young lady soon enough."

"Come with us, Teresa," Helena said. "Tomás knows the stars. They are the passion of his life."

Helena thought of his bed, pulled under the window of his room in her house. She imagined the little boy wandering through the night guided by a map that only he could see, while his brothers hunted frogs under the luminous umbrella of stars.

Her heart was full of tenderness for that child.

CHAPTER 19

✦ ✦ ✦

THEY SET OUT AFTER SUPPER. The children wore heavy clothing under short oilcloth ponchos that Teresa unearthed from yet another cupboard. Ponchos nearly dragging in the dirt, bedrolls hitched on to little shoulders, the children looked like the last soldiers in a long, sad war. Only their voices, piping over the call of frogs deep in an irrigation ditch, betrayed the exciting journey they were about to take.

Teresa sent them off from the back courtyard, after a last pleading from Luis, who wound himself around her knees and would not let go.

"Please come, Cousin Teresa, please come."

"Now, now. Someone has to be standing by the stove to make hot cocoa when you come home. You go take care of your mother for me."

She stroked his hair, then peeled him from her knees and gave his backside an affectionate pat as he ran to join his brother and cousin.

They did not walk long, just far enough that the children would feel they were truly out in the night. Still, when Helena looked back, the house seemed a distant ship on black water, turning slowly away from them. She shivered and Tomás looked down at her.

"You're cold. Should we go back?"

"Oh, no. The children are so excited to see your sky."

Tomás took off his jacket, laid it carefully over Helena's shoulders, called to the children.

"This is good, I think."

He gathered them around the telescope, helped them take off the bulky bedrolls. Helena, sitting on a thick blanket a little apart from the group, heard him clear his throat, as though preparing to deliver a classroom lecture.

"There are animals in the sky, strong and beautiful animals that my telescope will help you find. These animals guide little children through the night. When you know they are there, you only have to remember them, and you'll never be afraid again.

"The stars are always with us, night after night, through all the years. Think of it. When you grow up, when you are as big as I am, these same stars will still be there, shining for you just as they shine tonight. They have shone in the sky for all eternity. Imagine what they saw in the past and what they will see. Wonders here on earth and on other planets in our galaxy. Imagine what they will see long after we are gone.

"They have stories to tell. Before you go hunting for them, you must know their stories. We'll begin with the fierce lion that lives in the sky.

"Once upon a time, a huge lion lived on the moon. Can you imagine a lion on the moon? His roaring bounced off the barren landscape, echoing back to him. Every time he heard the answering roar, he thought it was another lion. He searched the gray crags and silent canyons, roaring and hearing, every time, an answer to his search. But there was no other lion, no other living beast.

"One night, after much roaring and searching, he finally understood that he was alone. He looked at the earth, hanging in his sky, and decided the answering roars were coming from the earth. And so, he turned himself into a fiery shooting star and flew to earth.

"He saw many creatures on earth, and for a time, he was happy. He roamed from place to place, looking for creatures. But, being a lion, he always roared a greeting. And people and animals ran from him in fright. He scared them so badly they finally went to their strongest warrior and told him, 'Something must be done. We cannot live with this lion in our midst. He is scaring us, making our children cry and our animals run and hide.'

"And the warrior, who was a god in disguise, knew he had to send the lion away. But he saw the lion for what he was, fierce but lonely. And so, he didn't send him back to the empty moon. He turned him into a beautiful constellation of stars and set him in the night sky. And there he remains to this day, surrounded by other animals made of stars and very happy."

Helena heard a little sigh from one of the children, a murmur of contentment at a story well told.

"Now, look through my telescope, and you will see the largest star of the beautiful lion, the one that shines the brightest. It is called Regulus. You must remember that name and remember why it is the biggest and brightest star. It is the lion's heart. Once you find the heart and know it well, then you can find the lion easily."

Helena watched Tomás lift Luis up to his telescope, whispering to him as the boy put his eye to the glass.

She looked at the two figures, one tall, one small, and asked God, who surely must be with them in the shining night, to bless her Luis, to give him a long life filled with curiosity and passion, with a love as strong as his teacher's for knowledge. She asked all this of God, knowing it was too much. Asked and saw Tomás gently set Luis down and lift José in his place.

Helena tipped her head back to find the lion's heart, then up and up until the land curved away under her. The earth was the fist of a child. The sky was God's own cupped hand, laid gently, protectively, over the small hand curled under it. She felt part of the night, lost in it, with only Tomás and his polished wooden telescope to guide them through the mysterious world they had entered.

She leaned back on her soft blanket, wandered through the stars without any conscious thought, lulled by the low voice of Tomás giving the children another story.

⬩ ⬩ ⬩

Luis was the first to get sleepy. Tomás brought him to Helena, who rolled him in one corner of her blanket and kissed him asleep.

Sibella was not far behind, saying she needed to take "a little nap beside Helena, too." José followed without any encouragement from Tomás. Helena relinquished her blanket and covered all three children with their own blankets.

"We'll have to wake them soon and get them into warm beds," she whispered as soon as they were tucked in.

"In a minute, Helena. Come look at Scorpius."

Tomás guided her to his telescope, his hand pressing lightly on the small of her back. She bent her head to the eyepiece. A dazzle of light greeted her.

"Do you see how his tail swings into the darkest part of the Milky Way? Some say the stinging tail sweeps open the entrance to Hell. He is the dark and the light, the lowly creature scuttling in the night, illuminated in one of the most spectacular gatherings of stars."

Helena drew her eye away from the glass.

"Did you find Antares? The largest star."

Helena looked again through the telescope, saw Antares shift into sharp focus at the same moment she felt Tomás' arms around her, adjusting the scope. She straightened up, gazed directly into the sky, leaning back slightly into the embrace of her children's teacher.

"And your girls with skirts of light? Are they here?" she whispered.

"My girls?"

"I saw them in your room."

"The Pleiades. They only show themselves for a few months. The rest of the year they're hidden from view, leaving us longing for them."

He fell silent as they looked out at the night sky. The stars were burning in the heavens, giving off cold trails of vapor, flaring the last of their light. Stuttering into the black void until they sparked out, one final burst of flame to be seen by yet another lonely child in some distant future.

Helena began to tremble. Tomás wrapped one arm around her waist, pulled her against him. She felt the bones of him like star points marking her body, mapping it for his own. His hand was on her throat, in her hair. She heard her name—"Helena"—nothing more, turned as stars wheeled overhead, lifted up her face to meet his lips.

The air was cold around them as they lay on hard, bare earth. Cold on her cheeks, her hair undone and wild around her, her hands gripping Tomás' arms as if she were dying. Cold on the mouth and neck he kissed. Cold on the moon-white breast he bared and stroked.

She arched convulsively under him, gave in to his weight. Threw back her head, saw all the stars recede into darkest night. God was not with them.

✦   ✦   ✦

Helena woke Luis first, lifted him, half-asleep, into her arms, smelled his sweet breath and warm skin. He was still hers. He had not been lost to her. She cradled him and, in his sleep, he wound one hand into her tangled hair. She carried him, wrapped in her blanket, back to his safe bed.

Tomás carried Sibella, who snuggled close against his neck. José walked silently beside Helena and remembered all he'd heard.

Chapter 20

+ + +

HELENA WOKE BOUND IN DAMP SHEETS. She was alone. She was not alone. The drums were with her. This time, she would not resist, would let the hollow vibrations lead her to whatever lay down the narrow hall.

Black surrounded her. She did not see. She followed rhythm and something else—voices, pure and high, chanting ancient hymns of sorrow.

Helena was pulled along the hallway as the drumming swelled, became wings thrumming in a small space, beating heavy air. Her white nightgown gave off no light, her small, bare feet did not feel carpet. Only her hands responded. Fists clenched at her side, knuckles brushing soft plaster, she passed one door frame, two, three, four—all closed, stoppered up against the sound.

She moved by instinct of bone and muscle, no thought of crying out, moved toward the frantic wings, the calling voices, and found, by memory alone, the frame of the deeply carved door.

She almost fell into the altar room. Her fingers, expecting solid wood, touched only air. She stumbled once, recovered and stood still. The drumming was all around her, like dark dancers pounding swollen bare soles on the hollow floor. The singing, a high lamentation, came from above.

Helena raised her eyes. And thought she saw the face of Célia peering down at her. Some scurrying movement up there, a break in the drumming pattern.

Suddenly, Helena was afraid. She backed up to the wall, fingers searching for the door frame. Felt a hand over her hand, a mouth at her ear.

"Don't startle her. She'll fall."

"Who..."

"It's Sibella, dear. I can coax her down."

Helena pressed her back flat against the wall to stop her trembling. Heard Teresa step away from her, heard her soothing voice talking to her granddaughter, perched high on the altar.

"Come down, my angel. Climb down now. Climb down. That's a good girl."

When Teresa carried Sibella into the hall, Helena saw the child was sound asleep.

✦ ✦ ✦

Teresa laid Sibella gently in her bed, then led Helena to the kitchen. She poured sweetened milk from a can into a battered kettle, stirred in coffee from the evening meal.

"I always find her in the altar room," Teresa said. "As long as we don't wake her, she never knows a thing about it the next morning. She'll be a little tired, that's all."

She handed Helena a large cup of white coffee, poured another for herself, sat at the table beside Helena and looked carefully at her face.

"You need to sleep now too."

Helena heard the dark wings, felt them pulsing in her veins.

"What was the drumming?"

"Just Sibella, dear, banging on the poor altar to some rhythm only she can hear. I think sometimes I should take out the altar, give the child a rest. But I worry what the gods would do."

"And the voices?" Helena asked.

Teresa looked at Helena, then away.

"Teresa?"

"You'll have to know the story then. If you heard the music, you'll have to hear the story of Célia."

Teresa stared through the thick kitchen windows, as if the old story were playing against the night curtain.

"She was a precious baby, they say. A child adored by both her parents, especially her father. When she was born, he almost worshipped her. Wouldn't let anyone, even her mother, keep Célia from him. He had to have her by his side from the time she was tiny. Had her riding with him until she was old enough to handle her own pony. Took her into the fields on days her mother could not persuade her father that a daughter's duty was at home.

"Everyone thought he would grow tired of her, would let her stay in the house once she was older. It was only proper. But he did not.

"He had other children. His sons worked with him, of course. He taught the boys everything they needed to know about growing crops, managing the cane and the slaves. The other girls, Célia's older sisters and younger, were left in their mother's care. Not Célia. Well, she was a beauty, as you know. And she adored her father. Sat by his chair evenings, brought him food when he did not want to face his family at the table. Some said their love was blessed; others said it was wicked. It was what it was, I suppose. We'll never know the answer to that. All we know is that one day he died."

Teresa took a sip of sweet coffee.

"Out in a cane field, all alone. Célia, for once, stayed in the kitchen to help her mother prepare food for a saint's day. When her father did not come home for his noon meal, they thought nothing of it. He often stayed away 'til dark and later. But when his horse appeared alone in the court-yard toward evening, they knew something dreadful had happened.

"His sons went out to look for him in the fading light, then went back out with slaves bearing torches. Three slaves found him lying on his back between two rows of cane, two rows that looked just the same as every other row. Nothing to show why those canes would be the last bits of green he saw on God's earth.

"His own machete was in his thigh, nearly splitting it in two. They put him on a litter and dragged him through his fields and home with his machete still in his leg.

"Some said the slaves who found him had killed him. How else could they discover him in the dark among rows and rows of sugar cane? They were whipped but admitted nothing. When Célia heard of the whippings, she made her brothers stop, took in the three broken men, gave them work in the house.

"Others said he did it to himself, though I've never known a man could manage that. They said he knew he could not keep Célia forever to himself and wished to die instead."

"Something happened to her," Helena said. "You can see it in her face."

"When she finally understood her father would not come back, she chose to enter a convent. Her mother thought it best. She did make one last request, that Célia not leave until a portrait had been painted.

"The artist who did her portrait was not known. He just appeared one day as they do, looking for work, hoping to make something last through the winter. He probably smelled of turpentine. He was riding a sad horse that was half-starved.

"Célia's mother took him in and told him to sketch her daughter, gave him charcoal and good paper from Célia's own art box. When he finished the sketch, Célia's mother saw he was good, better than she had expected. What she did not see was the dark side of the man, locked away behind a handsome face.

"He made few requests—a room with good light, nourishing meals and whiskey. He did not ask to be left alone with Célia. Her mother would not have allowed that.

"He worked four months on the portrait, small as it is. Four months. Can you imagine? Well, you probably can, being the painter of the family.

"Then he left, after the rains were over and the sugar cane was growing sweet and tall. Célia's mother was pleased with the painting, even though it meant telling her daughter good-bye. A message was sent to the sisters that Célia was ready to be received into the arms of Jesus. Her grief had not abated. If anything, it seemed stronger.

"She waited for word from her order. Word never came.

"The good sisters knew and her mother guessed. Célia denied she was pregnant. Who knows? Maybe she didn't understand what was happening to her. Or maybe she thought she could will it away or pray to God in her convent and have it taken from her somehow. That didn't happen, or maybe it did.

"Célia's mother shut the poor girl up in her room, cursed the artist who had defiled her, sent horsemen out who should have been overseeing crops to search for the wretched man.

"They never found him. No one had seen him, heard of him or hired him. He had walked out of this house and disappeared into the clean summer air.

"Rewards were offered, even though Célia begged her mother to leave it be. Men came to the house with a hat or a piece of torn leather they claimed was a rein from the painter's poor horse. Women came with tales of seeing a lone rider descend into the deepest part of the river and never ride out the other side. All were rejected.

"And Célia grew bigger and bigger. She gave birth to a son.

"He died in different ways. Some said he was left to starve, or claimed they saw marks on his throat. I believe he died in her womb. Why would Célia's father make her kill her own child just to have her back? The child was still-born, I say."

Teresa sat silent. Helena waited, seeing before her the haunted eyes of a young girl.

"And Célia?"

"No one knows. She disappeared from all the household records without a mention. She may have wandered off or lived years closed away. Her father was in no hurry. What is a woman's lifetime balanced against all eternity? He knew that he would have her by his side. And so he does. But when she remembers, from time to time, the son she almost had and loved, she comes back."

"Why didn't I see her portrait on my last visit? I would have remembered it."

"I hid it. It was around that time my son brought baby Sibella home. We don't let Célia see the infants."

The two women sat together for a time in the quiet kitchen. Early morning light, diffused and welcome, seeped through the watery windows and around the edges of the old wooden door frame. Acceptance born of sorrow sat at the table with them. Célia would rest for a while.

Chapter 21

+ + +

St. John's feast day fell in the middle of Helena's last week at the plantation. Teresa decreed that the celebration, a riot of bonfires, dancing, eating and sky rockets, would not be held until Roberto could come.

"He needs a dance before heading back to that dungeon of a factory," she said.

The younger workers held their tongues, but the old field hands, who had been with Teresa all of their lives, grumbled at having their holiday postponed.

"Let them grouse," Teresa said. "The old men will start drinking when they want to anyway and will be in need of a good meal by Saturday."

The rest of the house was thrown into an orgy of preparations. Wood was stacked into four large pyramids beyond the courtyard and covered with canvas tarpaulins to keep it dry. Antonio unearthed a crate of fireworks and put two men to work selecting the best and biggest for the festival.

Fresh corn, always offered to St. John, was prepared by two field workers' wives. The sweet smell of corn cooking in coconut milk soon filled the house and everyone's nostrils.

Teresa sent out messages to her sons, holed up in city jobs and playing at university, to come home for the party. No one could refuse her.

"They'd never turn down a dance and barbecue," she said. "This will give me a chance to see if Evandro's silly wife has finally gotten herself pregnant."

◆　◆　◆

Marcos, Teresa's oldest son and Sibella's father, arrived on Friday morning with a girlfriend, sending Sibella into a jealous frenzy. She sulked, threw herself at her father, tortured poor Luis by making up intricate games he couldn't follow and then taunting him with "Baby" when he began crying in frustration.

Helena, finding Luis in tears and getting no coherent explanation, led him up to his room and made him lie down with a cool cloth on his forehead. When she returned to his room a little later to check on him, she found José lying next to him on the bed. She took them both down to the kitchen for tastes from Teresa's black pots.

Teresa looked at two forlorn faces. Luis' eyes were still puffy from crying.

"I need some big boys to help me put up decorations," she said.

The boys followed a maid lugging a long wooden ladder outside and soon were unfurling shiny paper flags to hang on wires strung around the courtyard.

Sibella, missing since her early-morning fight with Luis, appeared suddenly in the kitchen with her flushed face dirty and her hair disheveled. She had two young uncles in tow. Both gave their surprised mother hugs.

"How did you get here this early? The mail boat isn't due yet," Teresa said and then spotted Sibella.

"What have you done to this child? You boys, off on some adventure before you even come in to give your poor old mother a kiss."

"They found an old man with a leaky boat to paddle them up here," Sibella said, adding when everyone started laughing, "They did too."

"I cannot tell a lie," Carlos, the younger uncle, said. "And neither can the fair Sibella. We just couldn't wait for the mail boat. What's for lunch?"

Roberto arrived on the mail boat with Teresa's son Evandro. Evandro's wife quickly found a pot to stir and tried to stay out of Teresa's way. Teresa raised one eyebrow in her direction, then went to embrace Roberto.

"I brought you a present," he said, grinning. Three men huddled in the courtyard doorway. All carried musical instruments.

"By God, we will have a celebration," Teresa said.

"Where's Helena?"

Teresa glanced at him.

"Go find her, would you? Lunch is almost ready."

✦   ✦   ✦

Helena and Tomás stood by her bedroom window, joined by sunlight. The room lay in shadow. Only the two silhouetted figures were framed by light. He bent over her, as though sheltering her body with his own.

Roberto found them together. Saw the teacher's hand on his wife's wrist. Saw them look up in unison, move quickly apart.

"Roberto," Helena said and then, in a rush, "We were looking at the portrait."

She was holding the painting of Célia. Roberto's boots, as he walked toward them, struck hard on the wooden floor.

"I said I don't want her in here."

He looked only at Helena.

"The light's best in here," Helena said quietly.

Roberto turned abruptly to Tomás.

"Leave," he said.

Tomás hurried out of the room.

Helena brushed past her husband to set the painting back on its easel. Roberto reached for her, gripped her arm.

"Everyone is waiting for you," he said.

◆ ◆ ◆

Célia was still there, huddled in her corner, when Roberto and Helena came to bed.

Roberto glanced into the corner.

"I told you I don't like this."

"It's only for a few more days."

"No, Helena." His voice rose, echoed in the quiet room. "No more. I forbid it."

"I did this for you. Tomás says I'm learning fast. He says..."

And then he was coming at her. She reached out, to touch him or stop him, she wasn't sure which. Saw his hand sharp in front of her. The long fingers extended flat.

She turned her head and he grabbed the braid twisted at the base of her neck. His fingers tangled in the braid, the thick coil pouring loose in his hand as he tightened his grasp. He jerked her up short, as though she were a horse to be broken. She stood very still, not breathing, looking straight out into the black of a suddenly airless room. Heard Roberto groan as he pushed her face down onto the bed. Rolled over and found only darkness.

For one moment, she thought her husband had left her.

He was in the corner. There was a tearing sound. She screamed, as though his knife had gone not through Célia's face but into her own. Then he was standing over her, standing over her. And then he was gone.

Chapter 22

✦ ✦ ✦

Saturday dawned high and bright, all rain banished in honor of St. John and his delayed feast day. By midday, friends from neighboring plantations were arriving on horseback and by buggy, bringing cakes and corn confections, jugs of homemade rum.

No formal lunch was served. People came into Teresa's kitchen, found a chunk of cheese or a rosy mango to eat, lifted lids to inhale clouds of sweet steam, opened the forbidden oven door to peek at rising cakes, all over Teresa's protests and swats.

The celebration rose up in the afternoon, gathered itself like a woman pulling up her skirts for a fast dance, and ran headlong into the rest of the day.

Two of Teresa's women stood at the kitchen table, stirring batter for more cakes, mixing salads, sprinkling corn croquettes with bread crumbs and laying them in a large cast iron skillet for frying. The huge kitchen fireplace, usually quiet behind its screen, raged with a fierce fire. A hog turning on a spit in the fireplace's jaws spattered grease into the hissing flames.

The children, joined by a gang of newcomers, ran in and out of the kitchen, banging doors, sticking fingers in pots, stuffing pieces of cake filched from the table into their mouths. Teresa threw out orders to her kitchen help, hauled a kettle out of the fire onto the hearth, shooed children away from her feet, swept back hair flying out of her bun.

Out in the courtyard, the musicians, fortified with an endless stream of beer and rum, took up their instruments. The band's leader unsnapped the leather straps on his accordion, let it draw in one long breath and began playing a heart-jolting tune. Roberto and his cousins, back from a noisy ride through the cane fields, heaped plates high with shredded beef and onions, farofa and beans. There was a round of beer, followed by shots of rum and more songs.

"At this rate, we'll all be dead by nightfall," Teresa said, looking fondly at the men through the open courtyard door.

Helena, slicing fruit into a large bowl, tried to apologize for the damage inflicted on Célia.

"Nonsense," Teresa said. "What happened couldn't be stopped. I shouldn't have let you choose her, that's all."

"Let me send her to the city for repair."

"She'll be fine. She always has been. Here, take this pot out to the courtyard to let it cool. But keep those boys away from it. They'll eat everything before the party starts if I let them."

A series of loud bangs greeted Helena's entrance into the courtyard. The band stopped dead. Somewhere, someone answered the blasts with a volley of gunfire. A sky rocket streaked high above a field as swearing drifted over the courtyard.

Helena went to her husband, whispered, "Teresa says Célia will be fine."

He looked at her without expression, turned back to the men at the table.

✦ ✦ ✦

Night came on. Voices got louder. Food was carried to the courtyard table on large platters and devoured as soon as it arrived. Before the crowd reduced the first hog to slivers, a second was set turning on an open pit near the courtyard. The smell of roasting pork mingled with loud laughter and music.

The band finished a long ballad about a cowboy down on his luck. A drumbeat swelled out over the throng. The accordion player, swaying a little from emotion and rum and grinning like a madman, launched into a song of devilish love and dishonor.

The table was carried to one side. Bathed in the band's music, couples began recalling the old steps, slapping feet in time to the drum and triangle. The children, wearing long capes, ran in and around the sweating, laughing dancers.

Teresa sent men out to light the bonfires with long torches. Flames streamed behind the men as they approached the pyramids of wood, then shot straight up as the fires caught hold. Several couples danced in the dirt beyond the courtyard, kicking up dust that rose to meet smoke and sparks from the fires.

A group of children, squatting by a fire for light and warmth, tucked fat candles inside tiny paper parachutes and lit them. The white chutes, puffed by hot air from the candles, climbed the air over the courtyard, glowing quietly, then burst into flames one by one and plummeted.

Teresa and Helena carried out a steaming kettle of hot rum, laced with lime and spices, and ladled it out to the dancers. More bottles of beer were opened. The dancers jostled each other, drank without missing a step.

A man Helena did not know approached her with his hand out. Helena looked at Teresa.

"Go dance," Teresa said. "You've done enough."

Helena danced with him, one fast tune and then a second. Someone cut in, another stranger, and she danced with him until the band's drum slowed, taking up the beat for an ancient song. The triangle player began singing, in a falsetto, the timeless words of yearning and sadness.

"Oh, my sweet darling, don't ever leave me.

Where will my heart go, if you don't stay?

Oh, little darling, how will I stand up

on the next morning, if you go away."

Two lines formed, men on one side, women on the other, gliding back and forth, back and forth. The line of women moved to the men, skirts swirling, then retreated, tempting the men to follow them. Fireworks bloomed overhead— red, silver, cobalt blue, magenta.

Helena could see no one she knew — not Teresa, not Teresa's sons. Her own boys had disappeared, their teacher perhaps with them, perhaps not. Her husband was gone, lost among the faceless men who danced around her. What happened tonight would happen.

She danced without thought, her feet moving on their own, her body carried like a speck of ash floating in the courtyard. The shifting lines blurred as men and women joined for a brief duet, then turned again and again to someone new.

Helena curtsied in unison with the women on either side of her, danced to a man in a black leather hat with a flat brim. Fireworks unfolded above his head like giant flowers of the jungle. Smoke drifted over the courtyard, caught in the women's fanning skirts. Helena circled her partner as he reached for her waist. She spun closer and he pulled her in roughly. She looked up, startled, and saw her husband's dark eyes staring down at her.

She danced away from him. The line of women moved forward. She linked arms with her next partner and saw another woman in Roberto's arms.

It seemed the music would never stop. It seemed it would stop and she would find herself embraced by a stranger, swept away into the smoky night by someone she could not see or name.

She danced until she had no memory of not dancing. Danced without hope. Swayed in and out of the line of men like a dream, like a nightmare.

Danced until she faced her husband once again.

She linked arms with him, turned into his embrace. Saw he was gazing somewhere beyond her. Moving as though utterly alone. He spun her out in front of him. She caught a glimpse of his face and thought she saw something giving way, some momentary tenderness. He pulled her back into his arms. They stood still. Dancers swirled around them. Smoke from the dying fires eddied at their feet, mixed with a strange warm wind blown suddenly across the dark courtyard. It smelled of old earth stirred again by green shoots, coals brought to life one last time.

Helena bowed her head, rested her forehead on her husband's chest, her arms tucked between them. She felt him look down at her at last. She lifted her face to him and whispered, "Please take us home."

Chapter 23

✦ ✦ ✦

The yellow house was opened up, aired out after Helena's long absence, as though with her gone no one had lived there. Though the cook had been busy in the kitchen and the maids had swept and cleaned for Roberto, the rooms smelled musty and neglected without Helena.

She felt she had been away years. Away or asleep or ill. Now she thought she was reviving. She opened shutters, dusted and scrubbed alongside her giggling maids, cleaning every surface to cleanse herself.

The house was small after the endless hallways and empty rooms of the plantation house. It could hold a person, wrap itself around her and keep her safe. If Helena could make it gleam again, shine as it had when she first came to Esperança, a young and blameless bride, all would be well. The house would take her back. Nothing would have to change.

When the scrubbing and polishing were finished, word went out along the river that Helena needed a photographer.

Word came back. A photographer was traveling with a small circus more than a day out of Esperança. He would come ahead, take the pictures she needed for her portrait, rejoin the circus when it arrived in Esperança.

He arrived with a chill wind that swept through the little dirt square of Esperança, made palm trees shiver, sent leaves scattering down the forlorn and empty dirt streets. The rainy season, lingering beyond anyone's memory, had finally driven the townspeople inside where they watched their mud walls sweat and prayed their houses would still stand in the morning. The river, swollen and dirty, heaved and rolled in its banks like a horse in labor. Cracks in the earth filled with brown, surging water, forming creeks where none had flowed before. When the rain let up, for an hour or a day, the muddy earth looked torn and spent.

The photographer appeared at the south end of town, where the main street bled out into trackless land. He walked in, leading a donkey pulling a small caravan striped with bright rays shooting from a large winking eye. He walked straight to the yellow house, looking neither left nor right, came to the gate, clapped his hands twice and brought a maid running from the kitchen.

It was mid-morning. Roberto was in his factory, watching over the large kettles of concrete turning as slowly as the world. The children were at their lessons, restless after their days in the plantation sun and repentant under their mother's serious looks. Each of them knew, in his small boy's heart, that he must have done something to make Helena sad.

Helena was in her bedroom, reading, for the second time that morning, a small scrap of paper she had found wedged into the inner door frame of her bedroom.

"Come away," it said.

The paper was unknown, a corner ripped in haste from a larger sheet, a corner much like the pieces Helena stole as a child from Os Olhos de Michelangelo.

"Come away. Shed your dusty clothes and water my fields with your fresh body."

The handwriting was as familiar to Helena as her own palm. She brought the paper to her face, breathed in the smell of warm grain, old leaves and the hand that had so recently held it. Inhaled the scent of skin and intimacy one last time. Crumpled the paper into a tiny ball, dropped it deep in her skirt pocket. And went downstairs to meet the photographer now standing boldly in her vestibule, staring into the face of Gabriel.

◆ ◆ ◆

The photographer unpacked his large camera the next morning, balanced it like a heavy insect on its spindly black tripod legs in the courtyard. Rain threatened to burst through the overcast sky. No matter, he said. He needed whatever light there was.

Two maids carried Roberto's dining room chair into the courtyard. Roberto, already late for work and looking vexed, sat in the throne-like chair. Luis stood to his right, exactly as Helena had pictured the pose in her mind, leaning into his papa's shoulder and looking happy to be so close. José stood to Roberto's left, a little apart, though

Helena urged him closer. He gazed straight at the camera, looking unafraid but uncertain of his place in the portrait.

Helena stood beside the photographer, seeing how the scene would play out in her portrait, trying out colors in her mind, thinking how to lay the shadows across the dark contours of her husband's face, how to bathe her son's face in sunlight so it glowed like a Leonardo angel.

The photographer ducked under his black cloth.

Tomás, standing slightly behind Helena, directed the children as the photographer changed plates several times, urging them to turn left or right, look at him, smile. Roberto glowered, barely containing himself while the photographer disappeared under his black cloth once more, then stood up abruptly as soon as he reappeared.

"Enough," he said, and left the courtyard.

"I can take several of the boys alone," the photographer said.

"Yes, good," Helena said and hurried into the house after Roberto.

When she returned, both boys were stuffed in the large arm chair, giggling. The photographer made two more plates, stopped.

"Now you," he said to Helena.

"Oh, no. That won't be necessary."

"You'll want these, Senhora. I won't be back this way."

✦ ✦ ✦

The circus arrived in Esperança that afternoon, and the photographer left Helena's house after lunch to rejoin it.

"Come see me tomorrow," he told her. "I will have your photographs for you."

As soon as he was out of Helena's gate, Luis asked to go to the circus. Then, hearing a surprising refusal from Helena, began begging.

"Please, Mama. I'll be good."

Luis had gone to the circus when he was four, the only other time it had come to Esperança in his short life. He did not remember the nightmares of screaming cats and hissing snakes he had suffered for weeks afterwards.

José had never been inside the big tent, had seen only what he could glimpse as people streamed past him into it. He remembered the smell of frying pork his mother was selling from a small charcoal brazier set in the dirt outside the tent. He remembered dancing colors, the neighing and stomping of unseen horses. He remembered a tiny figure flying through the air with scarlet legs and a body that sparked flame like the chandelier in Helena's dining room.

"Let them go," Roberto told Helena that night. "They should see the bareback riders and big cats."

"We need to be home. The nights are too dark here," Helena said, and Roberto did not question her.

The next morning, Luis had not forgotten. He stood next to Helena's chair after breakfast and whispered into her ear.

"If you let me go, I won't be afraid."

"Of course you wouldn't be afraid," Helena said, gathering him onto her lap. "You're my brave boy."

She kissed him all over his earnest little face and then whispered, "Run tell José that we'll go see the photographer this afternoon. You can see the prancing horses practicing in their ring."

✦ ✦ ✦

The circus had camped at the edge of town near the river, close to the fishermen's houses and the water needed for the animals. In spite of the rain and mud and threat of slides into the swollen river, they had perched their small caravans on the banks. The canvas tent, with a lone flag flapping from its pinnacle, was up, filled with wooden bleachers hugging a dirt arena.

Three horses were tethered to stakes near the tent. No wild cats were in sight, just a barred wagon full of gray doves that fluttered to the top of their cage when the boys passed. A popcorn wagon stood silent, waiting for hot oil and the night's crowd. A woman in a plain brown dress sat next to it, peeling and slicing onions into an iron skillet sitting on a brazier.

They wandered through the caravans. A bare-chested man, slathering white makeup over his face and torso, didn't look up from his mirrored dressing table when they passed. Another man, dressed in a faded black suit, juggled three Indian machetes high into the air. The boys stopped to watch, mouths open, then ran to catch up with Helena.

She was talking to a woman in a pink sweater and blue spangled tights, smoking a small cigar. The woman took the cigar from her chapped lips, used it to point out the photographer's striped caravan.

"He's waiting for you," she said, her face half-hidden by her drifting smoke.

Chapter 24

✦ ✦ ✦

It was Helena who discovered Luis was not in his bed. She had stayed up late, looking again at the black and white photographs lying in a row on her bed, including two of herself. In the first, she sat in a still white light, looking utterly alone. In the second, she had moved slightly and was a ghost in the light. She couldn't imagine why the photographer had printed the plate. She tore both into small pieces.

She gathered up the remaining photographs carefully, placing her favorite on top—Luis' face in full light, radiant as though blessed, looking at his father with eyes shining with open love.

She pulled out the bottom drawer of her dresser, empty except for a rose petal sachet Teresa had given her, thinking to store the photographs there until she started the portrait. Tucked underneath the innocent sachet, she saw a piece of thick white paper. She unfolded it.

"Come away," it said. "Come away and I will play you at dark, a silent bow drawn across your tender violin."

She read no further, crushed the paper, pushed it into the pocket of her dressing gown and discovered another note hidden there. She opened it.

"Come away. Meet me at the river and I will swim you, swim the length of you..."

She walked quickly to the small porcelain sink in a corner of her room. She placed each of the crumpled balls of paper into the bottom of the sink, added the torn photographs. Reached to the shelf above the sink, found the long matches and struck one. She touched each paper lying in the white sink as though anointing them and watched them burn to gray ash. A light piece of ash drifted up into the high, dark ceiling of her room as though willing her to follow.

She would not follow. She would burn out every impulse in her body, submit to the fire until she was hollowed out, purified, blameless once again. God would see her struggle and be placated. She prayed it would be enough.

She waited until the notes had burned completely, washed the last ashes away. Then she placed her photographs in the bottom drawer, looked at her reflection in the gilt-edged mirror over the dresser, smoothed back several stray hairs from her flushed face and walked down the hall to kiss her sleeping son's sweet face.

When she realized his bed was empty, she fought down a sudden panic.

"Don't be silly. He's with José."

She went into Jose's bedroom and discovered another empty bed.

Carmelinha and Helena walked quickly through the house, looking in every room but two—the sleeping teacher's, which Helena passed without even turning her head in the direction of his door, and her husband's. When it was obvious the boys were not in the house, Helena stood in front of her husband's closed door. Carmelinha, looking at her mistress' white face, knocked softly, then left her.

Roberto was lying in the dark with his eyes open.

"They're at the circus," he said. He sat up and turned on the small tin bedside lamp.

"You let them go?"

He looked amused.

"They didn't ask, Helena. They're little boys."

"We have to find them," Helena said, trying to keep panic out of her voice. "I want them home."

Roberto threw back the coverlet, turned toward his clothes laid out neatly on a chair. Helena watched him begin dressing, slowly, deliberately, as if he were going to work in the middle of the night.

◆ ◆ ◆

The street was dark, no moon to guide their way. An occasional sliver of light from a kerosene lamp or bare bulb leaked out around the edges of a closed shutter. Otherwise, the street stretched black before Helena and Roberto. Even Dona Ana's bar was closed up, silent on its side of the square.

For days and nights after, the bar would fill with people and talk. The townspeople, even the God-fearing married women who never set foot in Dona Ana's except to buy a precious bottle of beer for their husbands' suppers, would gather to tell their versions of the night the circus came to Esperança.

Some would vow they had seen the couple walking through the town, felt a cold wind surround them as Sr. Machado, their patron, and his lovely Helena passed by them.

Others would swear over short glasses of rum that the circus acrobat had thrown himself off his trapeze in a spectacular somersault, then frozen in a crouch in the middle of the high air, nothing but dust swirls circling up as Helena's scream reached him. The second trapeze, they said, had swung out to him as though guided by an unseen hand. He had grabbed it just at the moment of plunging and saved himself.

In the days that followed, they would say they saw it coming. But now they were all at the circus, laughing at the clown dressed like a baby sucking on a huge nipple. High overhead, the acrobat who would spin as morning broke on the edge of Helena's cry, waited on his small wooden perch.

Roberto and Helena walked without seeing, guided only by the yellow light and deep thrumming coming from the far end of town. The circus tent glowed like a fallen planet from the bank of the river. Helena, already holding her husband's arm, gripped it tightly.

"Something's happened."

"Helena, they're fine." But Roberto took longer strides, matching Helena's half-run toward the tent. It loomed over them, flickering light making it pulse as though alive. Cries floated out from under the canvas walls. Strange shadows lunged toward them, danced along the tent's edge. The crowd inside shouted in unison as a figure shot straight up, hovered for a moment in the dark reaches at the peak of the tent, then plummeted to the sound of a long moan.

Applause broke out, cheers. Under everything, the generator running the lights pumped like a dark heart.

Roberto moved ahead of Helena to the tent's open entrance. Vendors with the remnants of cooked food and small paper flags, flowers, birds, watched his approach. No one stopped him.

By the time Helena reached the tent's entrance, her husband was already starting down the dirt aisle between two sets of wooden bleachers. She saw a small child squatting motionless in the dirt next to the risers. She felt in one awful moment relief that a child was found, horror that there was only one.

She ran toward her husband as he touched the little boy's shoulder. The child turned slowly as though waking from a deep dream. Looked with his serious eyes at Helena running toward him, heard Roberto say, "Luis, son. Where's Luis?"

José turned to a spot almost under the bleachers.

"He's gone," he said, surprise in his voice.

He looked up at Helena, saw fear in her eyes, knew whatever had happened was his fault somehow. Tears started in his eyes.

"All right, son. All right," Roberto said gently. He crouched in the dirt beside José. "Did he say where he was going? Was he going to get some popcorn?"

José shook his head. Roberto stared into his little face for a moment, then stood.

"You two stay here in case he comes back. I'll walk the tent."

He left, looking as though he was forcing himself to slow down in front of the crowd, his workers.

Helena knelt in front of José, cupping his narrow shoulders in her hands.

"Look at me, José. Tell me where Luis went. I know you know."

"He was right here," José said in a shaky voice.

Helena stood up, leaving José at her feet. She searched the bleachers, telling herself that if she looked carefully into each face, she would find her son. She would tell herself he was there and he would be. God would see to it. God would find Luis and whisper in his ear to run to his mama.

A cloud of dust suddenly lifted from the small circus ring. The three horses she and the boys had seen in the afternoon walked into the ring. Each horse was blind-folded. Each carried a trussed and blindfolded rider lying lengthwise along his back. The horses began to trot as their riders, wrapped in white gauze as though bandaged, bent and writhed in balanced contortions on the horses' bare backs. The horses picked up speed, galloping around the small ring, mindless of the shrieks and clapping of the thrilled audience.

Helena wanted to scream at the horses to stop their mad, careening frenzy, wanted to shout at everyone to stop clapping and find her child.

When Roberto came up behind Helena from the opposite direction and touched her shoulder, she started, turned.
Saw he was alone. She grabbed the sleeve of his jacket,
began worrying it back and forth. He looked down at her
hand but did not stop her.

She realized what she was doing, forced herself to let go
of his sleeve. Said, "Do something."

"He must be outside."

"You looked everywhere? Are you sure?"

"Yes. You take José home. I'll find him."

"No."

"Go home, Helena."

Helena's head felt light, first her head and then her arms
and legs, weightless, as though she were being pulled by a
long, taut thread to the top of the tent, floating above the
crowd, small and transparent.

"I can't leave, Roberto. I can't."

José, still crouched in the dirt aisle, looked up at Helena,
fascinated. He had never heard this thin, high voice coming
from her white throat.

He knew that voice. He'd heard his own mother talk
to him in that voice the night before he left their house to
make his way alone to Helena's front gate. His mother had
told him to be brave and good. She had told him to forget
her. He had tried to obey her, tried to be good. But he had
failed. He hadn't watched Luis. He hadn't known he was
supposed to.

"Sit right here then," Roberto said.

Several people at the end of the bleacher, suddenly
aware that their patron and his wife were standing next to

them, slid down the bench, squeezed together in the sti-fling, dusty air, to make a space for Helena and José. Helena shook her head, lifted José onto the bench.

"I can see better standing. He can find me."

From his perch in the bleachers, José watched a man with a bright green face toss five golden balls into the air. The balls floated in front of the man's face, then rolled up his right arm and across his shoulders one by one until he held them all in his left hand. They were still for a moment, sheltered in the man's large hand, then began tumbling over each other, pulsing one by one from his outstretched palm, until they spun in the air like tiny moons in the tent's bright heavens.

He coaxed the balls back to his hands, brought them to his face, fanned his fingers out wide, blew gently. The balls flew straight out at José. He ducked, along with several other laughing people sitting near him. When he raised his head, the gold orbs had disappeared and Roberto was standing beside him.

"He went outside," Roberto said to Helena. "One of the vendors thinks she saw him leave. My foreman is here. He's rounding up men with lanterns. You take José home and wait there."

Roberto lifted José from the bleachers. José took Helena's cold hand. She did not look down at him, seemed to be looking nowhere. But she gripped his hand so tightly he thought his fingers might break. He didn't cry out, didn't make any move to pull his hand away.

He hurried out of the tent with her, away from the light and into the quiet town. The sounds of the circus were in his head. He heard sharp music, hissing lights, the screams and sighs of big-breathed animals he had never imagined. He saw only black. He had lost Luis.

He had looked away for just a minute, looked away to see the birds with iridescent wings flying overhead. They wheeled in the air above him, swooped low together, became the body of a silver-haired woman. She was naked except for the glittering mass of hair that flowed straight back from her forehead. She hung in the air above them, crying out in a strange, shivery voice words from a lost language.

He had heard Luis humming softly beside him, humming a river song. His hair drifting gently among the reeds, his hand riding the dark current of deep water.

José had looked away. There was so much to see, so much he hadn't known was in the world. The man with transparent skin whose blood pulsed through thin veins over pink muscle. The woman appearing suddenly on all fours in the middle of the dusty ring, as though born of the dust itself, circling the ring snarling and spitting, revealing a long, thick and spiny yellow tail.

And the eyes of his mother.

Oh, yes. He had seen his mother. He knew it was her, crouched by the open flap of the tent, head bent over the dark-red coals of her little brazier while the skewers of meat sizzled and popped in the heat.

José and Luis had hesitated at the tent's opening, peeking into the forbidden world calling them in. They had hung back until José heard a low voice beside him say, "Go in. I won't tell." He felt the whispering voice echo in his own throat. Looked into what he knew were his mother's eyes, then ran with Luis through the opening into the tent's dazzle.

✦ ✦ ✦

José stumbled down the rough street, pulled along by Helena. As if home would be any solace, as if Luis might be there suddenly, magically safe in his own bed. José wished it so, prayed to the god he imagined hanging in a somehow blue, blue sky. He knew it would not happen. He had seen the dark eyes of his mother sparked with glints from her coal fire. Still, he prayed.

His prayers were cut off by a strange light coming toward them, a light jerking up high in the dark, flashing down to illuminate the dirt street, blinking out for an instant, then swinging crazily up again into his eyes.

José clutched Helena's hand tighter as he saw the light was coming directly at them. It was accompanied by a terrible rasping sound, like a strange animal loose from the circus.

The light grew bigger, the sound louder, until it was right on top of them.

It was Tomás, carrying a lantern. He stopped in front of them, reached for Helena and pulled her into his arms. Her hand was wrenched out of José's hand. José saw her push Tomás away, saw his teacher was crying.

Helena leaned into Tomás' face.

"Find Luis."

José watched his teacher hurry off into the night, felt his hand caught tightly again in Helena's hand, a grip to ward off whatever blow was coming.

Carmelinha met them at the gate, looked at Helena's face, saw then it was José whose hand she held.

"Get me a chair," Helena said.

Carmelinha and the cook carried a dining room chair into the vestibule. Helena sat down on the front edge of the chair, grasped the arms as though willing herself to stay seated.

José, forgotten, stood by the back wall of the vestibule, looking at Helena's frozen profile, feeling the wings of Gabriel swinging over him, reaching out to the woman poised at the edge of the night.

Then a hand was laid firmly on José's small shoulder, and the cook led him to his bed.

Chapter 25

✦ ✦ ✦

Jose woke to a strange song. It rose higher and higher, no beginning, no end to this song of pain. He was floating into the sound, his blood pounding in his ears. He pushed up from his bed, bare feet on cold tile, into the murky hallway. Shining birds were swimming through bright circus air, golden balls hovering in the light. The acrobat was spinning on the high note of Helena's song.

She broke into sobs as José peeked around the corner into Luis' room.

Carmelinha was there with two other maids, the three of them bending over Helena, lifting her up, leading her away from Luis' bed though her arms still reached back for him. Half-carrying her down the hall to her own room.

José crept into the room. Luis was lying on top of his bedclothes in his shirt and shorts. His white feet were bare. His eyes were closed. His arm hung off the side of the bed. His hand, limp, looked almost blue in its whiteness. Thin tendrils of magenta reed with tiny bulbous flowers were still wrapped around his fingers, as though he had been picking a bouquet for Helena. His hair trailed across the damp pillow where his head lay.

José hunched inside the door, his back against the wall, and focused on Luis' face through the moans now coming from Helena's room.

"Get up," he whispered. "You get up right now. She wants you to."

He stared at the body lying on the short white bed.

"Get up now," he said softly.

✦ ✦ ✦

He was still crouched near the door when voices suddenly entered the room. Men were standing in the hall. The scent of water—thick, green—filled Luis' room. Fishermen were in the upstairs hallway, come in the name of death to accept their due and pay their respects, come to tell their stories to the grieving family and to each other.

"We went out with the lanterns. It was darker than I ever saw. The moon, where was the moon? Gone."

"I held the light up over the water, but it was hopeless. I said, 'God, if you ever hear a man's prayer, hear this one. Help me find the boy.' But the water was heavy as the earth."

"We looked down in the water. There was a light shining up from the dark of the water, I swear to you. A white light like God's hand itself was down there. Pulling the boy up, pulling him up with his hair all streaming behind and his arms and legs hanging down and tangled in awful weeds like I've never seen before and pray I never see again."

"I reached into the water and held on, and he floated up like the little flower that he is."

Ordinary men, they were used to ordinary deaths— babies dead before they took one full breath, women dead with babies still clinging to their wombs, brothers and fathers lost to waves and dust and knives. Ordinary deaths, not the terrible sight of God pulling a fallen boy from unholy water with his sure hand.

And then they were in the room, and Roberto was with them. The room was full of people, fishermen and their quiet, staring wives. They were crowding around Luis' bed, touching his white arms and legs, as though he were one of them.

José did not move. No one took notice of him. Roberto went to Luis, parting the group around his son's bed. He bent over him for a moment, whispering to him, smoothed his damp hair off his face, then straightened abruptly, thanked the townspeople for coming and stared into a space in the middle of the room until they fled.

When they were gone, Roberto sank onto Luis' bed, his face in his hands. After a long moment, he put one hand out and began stroking his son's foot over and over. José watched, knowing he was seeing something secret.

The cook, come to tell Roberto that the priest had been located in another town and ridden straight through on someone's poor horse, found José huddled against the wall. She pulled him up by one arm, took him back to his room.

"You stay here now and be good," she told him. "You pray for your poor little brother."

José prayed. He lay in his bed, under the sheet, and prayed for Luis to get up. He prayed for himself to be good, to be the best boy he'd ever been.

♦ ♦ ♦

They buried Luis the next evening, after a day of inconsolable sunshine to match the hot day he had been born. Teresa arrived mid-afternoon, bringing Sibella and two women from her own house to help with the cooking. Townspeople filed into the house, gawking at the furnishings, bringing the best food they could offer—small boiled river crabs, sticky jaca fruit, sour star apples, tiny red bananas looking like swollen fingers, soft sugar bread.

The food was heaped onto the scarred kitchen table. People drifted in and out of the hot kitchen, helping themselves to meats and pickled vegetables eaten with greasy fingers, adding their own offerings to the laden table.

Luis lay in the dining room, like his ancestors before him, in a coffin hastily cut in half to accommodate his small body and still tacky with white paint laid over the carved wood and gilt. The coffin maker kept a supply of coffins for adults who died without warning and several tiny, white coffins for the anjinhos, babies born dead or dying. There was nothing for boys of six. Boys who made it to six were strong. They had rebuffed the early diseases and ailments that carried away younger children. They lived into adulthood. When they did die, killed by starvation or drowning or the bad winds that sometimes swept across the arid land, they didn't receive the ornate caskets of the Machado family.

Luis lay quiet in his coffin, in the dark dining room, on the dark table. Decades later, traces of the paint from his coffin would still be visible on Helena's table. Anyone sitting at that table would know a child had lain there and would remember or wonder.

Helena sat dazed in one of the dining room chairs next to her son, dressed in a sooty black dress José had never seen. She made no movement, seemed incapable of movement, except for the slight murmuring of her lips as the townspeople filed past her, whispering ancient condolences, taking her hand, made bold by the grief weighing down the air around her.

Roberto stood beside her through that long day and greeted each person who came through his front door, thanked them formally for their courtesy, left them talking about his strength. Only José had seen him falter at his son's feet.

José sat at his brother's feet now, dressed in an identical suit to the one Luis was wearing. The suits made for their trip to the plantation, which now seemed long ago. José watched Sibella walking in and out of the dining room with her grandmother, saw her walk with Teresa to Luis' coffin and be lifted to kiss his cheek, saw her wipe her lips with the back of her hand as she was led back into the hallway.

She meant nothing to him now. She was a playmate from long ago. They had ridden imaginary and real horses, paddled in the bright water of Teresa's pool. They had eaten together, slept together, bathed together. Sibella had teased Luis and ignored him. He remembered the games they played, the sound of her laughter when she tormented them. Now he was done with her. She was from his childhood and it was over.

Teresa told him so. She took him from his chair beside the coffin, led him by the hand into the kitchen to give him food and lemonade and said, "You have to be the little man now. You have to be brave and good and take your brother's place. Helena needs you to be strong for her. No crying and no whining."

He nodded solemnly, trying to imagine ever taking Luis' place, trying to imagine that Helena would ever look at him as she had looked at Luis. He knew that it would not be. But he would try.

He was led back to the dining room, lifted to kiss his brother's dead cheek, amid the murmurs of the line still filing past Helena and Roberto. He took his place once again at the foot of Luis' coffin.

The room was hot. José was hot in his heavy suit. Luis must be hot too. He looked peaceful, his hair combed back and free of reeds, his eyes closed and his folded hands entwined with a rosary. But José knew he was hot. He knew they were going to close the coffin lid on him. Sibella said so.

"They shut it up and you'll never see him again," she whispered in his ear when they were eating breakfast at the long kitchen table, before the town came in through the front door and Carmelinha took him from the table and up to his room where his heavy suit and hard shoes waited.

"I saw my grandpa," Sibella said. "They shut him up and I never said goodbye. My father said I was an evil child because I wouldn't kiss him. It made my father cry, but I don't care. My father says it's your fault that Luis is dead."

José thought about Luis in the coffin with the lid shut. He knew Luis wouldn't be able to breathe. It was José's fault Luis had to be dressed in his hot suit and closed up in his coffin.

✦ ✦ ✦

In the early twilight of that long, hot day, children gathered in the vestibule of the yellow house, under the watchful eyes of Gabriel. Some of them carried bunches of marguerites. Luis' coffin was lifted from the dining table with its lid forever closed. José was led to the front of the children's procession. The children carried Luis through the town to the church.

José smelled the smells of little boys who an hour earlier had been playing soccer on the same streets, the smells of little girls scrubbed with soapy water from Luis' river. He heard the church bell ringing slowly out over the town. He heard the fisherman who had pulled Luis from the muddy Rio Branco say to anyone who hadn't heard, "I lifted up my lantern, and the brown water turned blue, and the blue water turned clear as God's eye. And there he was, lit by a glowing ember. God's eye was on him, poor sparrow, and God guided my hand."

José watched the priest, robed in embroidered vestments the townspeople hadn't seen since Helena's wedding day, intone a final prayer over Luis' closed coffin at the front of the sanctuary. He saw Helena, seated in front of him in the first pew, start suddenly as though shaken from a long dream, lift herself off the pew.

He knew where she was going. He could see it in the slant of her body, although he was behind her. He could feel the pull of her body to the coffin as though it were his body, not hers, that was longing to run to Luis, lift him from the small coffin, take him home.

José believed that Helena could do it. He knew she could tear open the coffin, even though it looked sealed for all eternity, bend over her son and breathe life back into him. She knew he wasn't dead. She could save him.

Roberto stood as she stood, gently pulled her back into the hard pew. She resisted him, then crumpled. When the service ended, she clung to his arm as they walked to their boy's coffin. Helena draped her body over it, hugging it as if to protect her boy from his awful journey. Roberto let her stay for a moment, then led her, blinded, out of the church.

CHAPTER 26

+ + +

TOMÁS MOVED THROUGH HIS DAYS ALONE, needing nothing, asking for nothing. He lived in Helena's grief as if it were his own. He thought it was.

He had loved the child Luis, because Luis was Helena's boy. He had led him gently into Teresa's pool, carried him when he was worn out from walking, taught him his letters and stories of the stars. He had encouraged him to look around the world with wonder, given him, he hoped, a good taste of life before he was led away.

He would miss the boy, surely. But he would carry on, teaching José, lying in his own straight cot at night, talking with his stars until Helena recovered. For she would, Tomás believed. He thought he knew what she would do. Because they had shared a night together, because they painted together and told each other secrets, he thought they shared a world.

He wished only to stay close to her. He would be content, he said to himself, to smell the perfume of her clothes and her breath, to breathe the air she had walked through, to hear her voice whether she spoke to him or not. He told himself it would be enough.

And then he knew it would not be enough. He stood one night behind the yellow house, looking up into the stars with his telescope without seeing anything, staring into the night sky as though the stars might speak to him, send down their pale light to show him the way. He thought of his own childhood, of his years wandering free on moon-filled nights, moving from star to star.

In his young days, before university, with no books to instruct him and no guide, he had made up his own heroes of the sky. Soldiers striding with large helmets and larger swords, frogs leaping, palm fronds swaying lazily in a black breeze only he could feel, dogs and monsters and rearing horses with manes and tails of fire.

Tomás looked into the sky behind Helena's house. All was quiet until a small sound, a sob so delicate it was almost no sound at all, made him turn his gaze from his telescope. Helena was walking toward him, hands outstretched, carrying a small package. The gift, if that's what it was, was open, rice paper peeled back from the box like a flower with shredded petals hanging limp through her fingers. Red ribbons trailed from her hands. She came to him silently, thrust out her hands.

Tomás looked inside the box. And saw that it was empty. He stumbled backward, nearly toppling his delicate telescope. Turned to see what he had hit. Looked back and saw only darkness. Helena was not there. But he thought he heard her pleading, wordlessly, for him to take the pain from her. Helena asking him to take her away from this painful place, take her anywhere that would make her forget.

He almost cried from relief and happiness. The days of silence fell away. He saw them walking together to the river, the same river that had taken Luis. Helena carried nothing but the paint box. No one followed them. No one shouted or questioned. They boarded the boat that had carried Helena to her blameless school with her blameless life, the boat that had brought Tomás to the yellow house. They stepped gently up the plank and were gone from their life.

Helena needed him now. He must be very patient, taking up no space, no air, only waiting, waiting. And then she would suddenly see him, see him standing in front of her as she had never seen him before, and she would understand that only he could take her away from her torment.

Tomás heard, from his narrow bed at night, terrible moans from her room. He knew they were not for him. Knew, when she cried out, it was for her lost son. He thought he could turn her grief away. He did not know what tides grief creates, what pull it exerts along ocean floors, the undertows it births and the wild waves that wash away everything normal and right.

Helena moved in her sea of grief, walked the ocean floor, tasting only salty bitterness. Tomás stood quietly by, willing her to look at him.

He had no thoughts for José. He ate with him in the morning, took him to the classroom to read and draw, but took no real notice of him. José did not exist for Tomás. But, in the end, he took Tomás away from Helena.

✦   ✦   ✦

Five days after Luis' funeral, Roberto called Tomás to the dining room. When he got there, he found Teresa seated with her cousin at the old table.

"I've decided to send José away for a while," Roberto said. "I'd hoped my wife might want..." He stopped, glanced at Teresa, looked down for a moment.

"We will, of course, honor our promise to his mother that he be raised as our own son. The school boat will stop in two days. You will be on it. A place has been found in the city for you and the boy. You will go first to ready things. You will continue in my employ as José's teacher and guardian. I only ask that you educate him well and send me reports from time to time. He will be prepared for university as Luis would have been."

Tomás looked at Teresa. She looked past him, as if what was happening were already an event far in the past. Tomás read her eyes, saw what lay there but refused to recognize it. It couldn't happen this way.

"I'll talk to José," she said.

Tomás rose from the table, the table where he and Helena had sat so many days, sharing bread and butter and memories. He stood up knowing he would not be sitting at that table again. Ever.

It didn't matter, he thought. It did not matter. He walked to his room blindly, lay down on his bed without removing his shoes, lay down even though it was the middle of the day and he should be starting lessons for José soon. He pulled his coverlet over him, cold in spite of his black suit, his black socks and shoes.

He closed his eyes, saw again how he extended his hand to Helena as they climbed up the boat's plank. They were taking the boat's slow journey downriver, meandering past unknown fishermen throwing nets into the deep water. Fishermen who had never seen them before, did not care who they were or what had happened to them in the dark water upriver. Men who saw only a beautiful woman looking at the man beside her as though she had been drowning and he had pulled her free of the water's heavy embrace.

They were in the city, living on air and painting in a tiny apartment, an attic of wooden floors, mossy walls, dusty windows overlooking the port where Helena's father watched the world coming to his door.

He believed, as he had never believed anything before, more than the words on the pages of his first books, the sums in his head, the stars in his sky, that he would speak to Helena and she would come with him. He would see her, speak the words of his heart, and they would fly away together.

She refused to see him, took her meals in her bedroom until he left. The maids said it was because she was in mourning.

"Later, Sr. Tomás, not now. Not now."

Teresa said it was for the best, then pretended not to hear or notice when he asked her again if she would talk to Helena for him.

And so, he stepped out into the street alone, brown suitcase in one hand and his telescope case in the other. He walked one last time through the lonely dirt square with his heart banging in his chest. He walked up the plank, boarded the creaking boat to carry him back to the city. And knew, with a certainty that cut his breath painfully short, that he would always be alone.

He left his box of paints for Helena.

⋆　⋆　⋆

A week later, José followed Tomás, boarding the same school boat his teacher had taken. He was wearing his long pants and his hard shoes laced up tight. He was holding Roberto's hand. He had hoped Helena would walk to the boat with him. But when Carmelinha woke him in the dark, scrubbed his face with a wash cloth, tied his black shoe laces and led him downstairs, it was Roberto who waited for him.

Despite his fear at leaving, José was thrilled. He had never been alone with his father. He could scarcely hear what Roberto was saying to him as they hurried through the early morning street to the river.

"Be good," he thought he heard. "Study hard. I want good reports."

José kept his head down, looking at his black shoes going one in front of the other, beside the black shoes of his father down the dusty main street to the river. He dared glance at him only once, found that, although his words were stern, his face was kind.

They stood at the river. José held fast to Roberto's hand. He looked into the water, flowing fast and deep. He thought of Luis walking into the river, walking into a world of floating reeds and rushing water. He tried to make his eyes see deeper into the water, see under the water into the secrets of the river. He looked for a small face, a hand waving at him. The water did not part. No hand was extended. Luis was lost and it was José's fault.

He knew he had been bad—to listen to his mother, sitting on her heels by the inviting flap of the circus tent, to listen to her voice saying, "Go on in. I won't tell." If he hadn't listened, if he had turned away from the tent just then, Luis would be safe. He would be safe in his bed, and José would be in his bed in the yellow house, just waking up now, just walking down the stairs with Luis to breakfast and Helena's kisses.

He looked up at Roberto again, but he was staring out over the river, seeing pictures José couldn't see. José held fast to his hand, hoping the boat wouldn't turn the river bend, hoping Roberto would say, "It looks like we'll have to go back."

It could happen. Things like that happened.

Just as the school boat rounded the corner, Roberto bent down, whispered something José didn't hear. Then he dropped José's hand.

And José turned to face the long canoe stretching out in front of him and begin his new life.

Chapter 27

✦ ✦ ✦

AFTER TERESA LEFT, Helena started roaming the house. She ate nothing, grew pale and thin. The maids and the cook tried to take care of their mistress. But they had a house to manage. Helena gave them no directions, seemed not to hear or see them. She registered no reflection of them as they moved in and out of her room, bringing in hot teas and broths she did not drink, standing her up to sponge her arms and legs, change her nightgowns, wash her face and brush her hair.

At odd times, she would slip out of bed, be found standing dazed in Luis' room. A maid, sent to search for her, would find Helena looking as if she had no idea where she was or who was tugging at her arm. One morning, the cook, coming into the kitchen to start the morning fire, saw her wandering in the dirt courtyard behind the kitchen, calling not for Luis but for his pony. She was carrying the pony's halter.

More often, the maids found her in the vestibule, staring up at her Gabriel, transfixed, or stroking his robe as if it were velvet instead of hard clay. Townsfolk passing by the house would see the lady in a frightful state, hair knotted and wild, nightgown wrapped around her like a shroud. Some said they heard her talking to her terrible angel, asking him questions in a pitiful voice. Others swore they heard him answer. All made the sign of the cross as they backed away from the harsh yellow light that seemed to infuse the small room, morning and evening.

One morning a workman from Roberto's factory came to the kitchen door and, calling for the cook, told her, "Your lady's in the front hall, where everyone can see, kissing the feet of her saint." It took both the cook and Carmelinha to pull Helena away, flushed and crying, and lead her back to her bed.

The same worker told Roberto that his woman was seen "almost in the street, Senhor," weeping in her dressing gown.

Roberto brought two men home with him that evening and had them carry the heavy statue of Gabriel up to the tower. Helena did not cry or cry out as her angel was carried backwards up the tiny staircase to the tower room. She only appeared at the doorway of her bedroom, twisting her wrinkled nightgown in her hands until her husband, satisfied that his workers could finish the job, came down the stairs and found her there.

Frightening sounds were heard through the house that night, scraping of something heavy being dragged across a bare wooden floor, moans and panting, then periods of silence so deep that everyone not already awake was abruptly wakened by the stillness. Roberto, after lying rigid in his bed, threw back the damp sheet, lit a new white candle and stood at his wife's closed door. Everything was hushed, as if death itself stood inside the door. He started in, then heard Helena's ragged intake of air. He returned to his bed and slept a ravaged sleep full of fits and drops and long falls with no end.

When he woke with a start, it was late morning. The sun was up, but the house was quiet. He could hear no one moving, as though exhaustion from the last few weeks had finally driven them all to their beds for good. He hurried from his room, opened Helena's door, found her asleep in a tangle of sheets.

He crept downstairs, realizing for the first time that he could barely breathe without the sound of small voices in the kitchen, without the anticipation of small faces waiting at the table. He hadn't known. He hadn't known.

He walked into the kitchen, saw the cook was still in her dressing gown. Her hair was in a braid down her back, like his mother's in the morning. He sat down heavily in a wooden chair.

The cook brought him his coffee.

"Senhor, I'm sorry," she began. "One of the maids just quit and I..."

"Never mind," Roberto said. "Never mind."

He sat with his coffee but didn't drink it.

✦ ✦ ✦

Carmelinha was waiting for him when he returned from the factory that evening.

"She made us, senhor," she said, then burst into tears.

"Come now, girl, finish what you're saying."

"She made us take her bed into the tower. She shut herself up there and won't come out."

Overnight, or so it seemed to his workers, Roberto turned into a ghost. Before they heard the rumors, before they began dreading the night and stopping up their ears against the moans and cries from Helena's tower, they saw their patron, the rock of their lives, become gray and transparent. He was a dead man moving among them.

He came to the factory because he always had. He dressed, he ate, he walked the long solitary walk to his office cell. It made no difference to him if he did any of it. He remembered only that he must do it; he could not remember why. He endured the hours at the factory, counted them off as he watched the paddles' maddeningly slow circles through the lumpish concrete in the vats below him, stared from the small window of his office perch until it was time to go home.

His men tried not to look at him, but his pain was as obvious as a gash in his coat sleeve, ragged and beyond repair. They took to muttering oaths and prayers behind his back, as if he carried a spreading stain of death and disorder with him. He saw their sidelong glances, their discomfort. They made no impression on him. He alternated between working them hard and ignoring them.

He could not remember what his life before had been, could not recall what it felt like to have a young wife waiting for him, two boys shyly coming to greet him, a direction and purpose to his days. He could not make his life before

Luis' drowning seem real. It was a dream, something from a child's story. Life was only now, the endless turning of the gray cement, the dry bread and cheese he forced down with cold coffee for his lunch, the circling of the afternoon hours until he could go home again.

At home, dark shadows under his eyes, dark sweat stains ringing his white shirt, he found no respite. He had not eaten a proper supper since Luis' death, taken no food on the dining room table. He couldn't even stay in the room, rushed through to the kitchen so he didn't have to see the dining table with its white scrapes from Luis' coffin glowing against the wood as if rebuking him. He tried to eat, but his mind was only on the muffled movement in the tower.

One night, he found himself up against the tower door with no memory of having left his supper cooling on the kitchen table. He could hear Helena talking, pleading with someone.

"Tell me," she was saying. "Please tell me. Please."

He stood with his forehead against the door, listening to his wife's hoarse, rasping voice, a voice he recognized but would never have known she possessed. She sounded to him like his mother before she died.

He listened as long as he could stand it. Then he began knocking on the door, calling to Helena. Asking her to open the door to him, begging her to listen to him. The haunting voice continued without ceasing. She could not hear him. He called louder, knocked harder until he was beating on the door.

He beat it to shut out the terrible voice on the other side, to block out the noise in his own head, to hear the satisfying sound of something being broken, to hurt himself, to rescue himself and his wife.

He thought he could tear down the door, beat it with his bare hands until it fell in splinters, rush up the stairs to the tower room with its tiny window facing the direction of the sea and Helena's childhood home. The ripping of heavy wood off strong iron hinges would be satisfying. It might drive out Helena's rants, now rambling into a chant, "Take me too. Please. Take me. Please. Take me. Take me."

He pounded on the door until his own rasping breath matched his wife's. The pleading in the tower did not stop. Nothing moved. No one came to rescue him. No little maid appeared at the end of the hall. God stopped them all in their chairs around the kitchen table with their forks in hands poised over their plates. Stopped the words in their mouths and the blood flowing in their veins, turned them to stone against all thoughts of rescue or flight until Roberto slumped spent against the battered door.

A key. If the door was locked, and it was, there must be a key. He roused himself from a crouch against the door, stumbled down the hallway, stopped. He had no idea what he was looking for, what shape or size the key to Helena's tower would take. He couldn't remember ordering a lock for that door, couldn't think why he would have ordered one. The tower was meant to be a plaything, a pretty ornament for a child bride to dream in.

He turned back, sat down heavily in front of the tower door again. There was no key, no lock. There was only a door bolted somehow against him. He abandoned, in that moment, any thought of rescuing Helena or himself, abandoned everything. He simply sat until Carmelinha came fearfully to him, asking if he wanted anything from his cold supper. He went to bed and did not dream.

From then on, he didn't even go to the kitchen at night, did not greet his staff or take off his jacket or wash his face after his day in the dirty factory. He went straight to the tower door.

The door became his lover. He sat every night on the floor, one shoulder pressed against the door, imagining another tender shoulder, round with flesh, pressed into his. Sometimes, he leaned his head against the door. Sometimes, he placed one hand against its rough wood, as if it could warm him. Most often, he simply sat.

Carmelinha placed a small chair from Tomás' old room by the door. Roberto didn't recognize it, would not have recognized it even if it had been his own. It didn't matter to him whether he sat on the floor or in a chair. He sat in his chair, and he ate his dinner off a tray brought to him by a maid. Or, he didn't eat his dinner, simply left it on his lap until a maid came to retrieve the cold food.

He knew the maids went to Helena during the day. He knew they went through the door to wash her, change her clothes, coax her to eat something. Whichever maid carried up his dinner tray would report to him as if he were still the master, as if he, and not they, were in charge of his house.

"She is so thin, Senhor," they said. "So thin. Her bones poke right through her skin, so pale you can see into her veins. Pale, pale blood, Senhor. Something must be done."

He listened, always nodding politely, but did not hear them. He cared only to sit by Helena's door. Sit and listen to her moving inside her tower room, sometimes talking, sometimes not.

When there was movement behind the door, Roberto was silent. He could not understand most of what Helena said, could hear only mutterings and moans. But he was quiet when she spoke. When she was quiet, when it seemed she might be calmer, he spoke. He told his wife, and the silent air around him, of the secret longings of his life, times he had never talked to anyone about, not Helena, not Teresa, certainly not his father.

He told Helena of his wish to leave the factory and the town, to ride forever in the green fields of Teresa's plantation.

"I'm at home there," he said simply.

He told Helena about his mother's illness and his own.

"I got well, Helena, even though I lost her. I grew strong after she died. I had to."

Sometimes, he stroked the door. Caressed it with his fine, long fingers, now scarred from beating on the door. Sometimes, although he heard nothing, not even breathing, he thought Helena was listening. Sometimes, she was.

Chapter 28

✦ ✦ ✦

BEHIND HER DOOR, Helena heard her husband talking. The voice, a soft murmur through the battered wood, was soothing. She was drawn down her tower steps. She couldn't understand all of his words, couldn't concentrate long enough to follow her husband's stories. But she listened to his voice as though listening to her school nuns singing vespers in Latin, knowing the good and the pain were hidden in the music, the foreign words.

She did not mean to cause pain, thought at times Roberto should know this was not his fault. Sometimes, she wished he would leave her alone. Other times, she ran her hand down the door, as if the wood were her husband's smooth skin, as if he could feel her touch, the tender, bruised fingers of her cracked hands. She talked to him through her hands, saying words with her fingertips that she could not speak.

And so they sat, night after night, one locked out, one locked in, each unable to move.

✦ ✦ ✦

Helena had no memory of going into the tower. She had seen her boy dead in his bed and was carried straight to the tower and her punishment by God. She knew she was being punished for her sins, for taking another man into her heart, for turning her back on her husband and her beloved son. She knew she could not be forgiven. She wished to be punished. But she wanted the punishment to fall on her alone, not on Luis.

Luis' face was always before her, laughing, his eyes shining, his beautiful mouth open, his delicate skin as radiant as da Vinci's angel. Everything else in Helena's world was gray, fogged. On days a light broke through her dirty tower window, she was drawn to the rays even though they pained her—a glimpse of some happiness she could not remember.

The window was high in the wall. She had dragged her bed to that wall, stood on it to look out. In her tower, she was above the world of Esperança, higher than anything except the church's tall wooden cross. The cross seemed far away, too far for her touch. But the river, the river that brought her to this town, that left her here like a small fish washed up on its muddy banks, that gave her happiness and then took it cruelly away, the river rose in her mind.

She saw it boil into the sky, hover over the dry, brown landscape like a terrible promise, then collapse on Esperança. The deluge was so swift and so solid that the whole town was crushed and swept away, cleansed from the earth as though it never existed. She lived with this image and found strange comfort in it. As though being washed away, she would be cleansed too, rinsed clean for God and borne back to a time when she was pure and innocent.

It could not be. The river would never save her, never take her back home, though at times she could almost smell the ocean of her childhood home from her tiny window.

She was with her father at the seaside. He was bending over, hands on his knees, then crouching by a small tide pool, beckoning her to "Come look, daughter. See the world we have found here."

She knelt beside him, peered into the clear, calm water. Saw sand turned green in the water, strands of seaweed sequined with bubbles, silvery pebbles giving off glints of light, tiny starfish.

She had promised Luis they would go to the sea, find the same tide pools, swim in the same waves where her father had guided her, his strong, elegant hands holding her as she kicked her legs and pushed through the foaming water.

"We'll ride the waves, Luis. Like little boats."

"Like little boats," he said. "And I won't be afraid."

And so he was not. He struck out fearlessly, following a guide only his innocent eyes could see in the dark and was found dead with his hair full of weeds.

This Helena remembered. Waking slowly, drugged, as Carmelinha called to her from a great distance. Running down the silent hall to find her son in his small bed at last. Not in it, on it. Lying more still than sleep itself and garlanded with shining vines, bulbous and prehistoric. As if the sea had come for him.

An ancient lake had opened under the river floor and tried to swallow her son. God had granted her one wish— Luis' body, risen up from old, dark water. God had given back her boy and then left her all alone.

She would sacrifice everything to erase that moment. She would joyfully and without hesitation trade her life for her son's. She would give her life and more—she would give up ever having lived, on one condition—that it not make Luis sad.

She made that offer to her angel. She asked Gabriel over and over to turn back the world for a brief moment, the span of one short, insignificant life, to breathe sweet air back into Luis' innocent lungs. Gabriel could do this, not for her but for Luis.

He could erase the small blot of her life, take away the happiness of her own childhood, the excursions with her father on his docks, the joyful rides on long sea waves, the first years with Roberto, even Luis' conception and birth. She would give up every moment of his life with her— the tug of his round mouth on her breast, the downy feel of his sweet head cradled in her arm, his solemn blue gaze into her eyes as he lay beside her during their afternoon rests together. He gave her the purest, most helpless love she had ever known. She would give it all back.

She would travel back until she took no space on earth, saw nothing of beauty or light, dwelt only in a dark place. She would do it to bring her child to life. She would swim that shadowed water with him, place her mouth on his lips, breathe her last breath into him, lift him high with the last spasm of her strength, place him gently on the earth's wide hip and sink into everlasting night.

She felt she was there already. She knew day from night only by the sunlight occasionally piercing her window and by the sound of Roberto's voice. She could not say when he had been there last or when he would come again. But she knew it must be night if he was there. His visits gave a center to her grief, a point from which to start as each long day and night unspooled before her.

When she heard him, she crept down the stairs, sat and listened to the endless whisper of sin and guilt or forgiveness and redemption. She didn't know which and didn't care. She simply let the sound wash over her, the words unfold above her head and shower down in blessing or recrimination.

When Roberto was not with her, and sometimes when he was, Helena paced in her tower. At these times, she turned on her angel, angry or pleading, willing to do anything, willing to do nothing, begging over and over in her hoarse voice, "Tell me. Tell me what you want from me."

Gabriel would not speak to her.

When she had fled to the tower, she thought she could blot out the voice of the world and hear her angel's voice. In the long silence, she still believed he was trying to sing to her. Now she understood there was no song, no voice left for her. Still, she begged.

Gabriel had always been with her. From the time he was first shaped with the clay of her birthplace and sent her mother's maid screaming into the kitchen, he had sung to her.

Now he was silent. His eyes were hooded, his wings folded in sorrow or scorn.

✦ ✦ ✦

The days and nights continued. Each day was the same day. Each night was the same night, coming again and again as a gong repeats the same long, mournful note until it is chiming against itself. Helena heard the refrain and its distant echo. She moaned and cried against the sound, tore at her clothes, her once shining hair, her face and arms, until madness and its blessed forgetfulness seemed her only release.

And then, and then. A long night like any other. She crawled down her staircase, her braid matted, feet scratched and nightgown ripped, and sat on the bottom step to listen to the voice behind the door. She drew up her knees, rested her head on folded arms. Roberto was telling her a story. His voice was as constant as the waves washing over her small head when her father taught her to ride her own body through the ocean.

She saw her father's strong hands under the water, guided herself to them, knowing they would lift her up into the light, and heard her husband say, "Mama told me, 'You must bring it to me. You have to bring it to me or I will die. Give me something that you care for, Robertinho. You know what it is. Bring it to me.'

"I brought her everything I treasured—a little wooden boat brought from the sea by my uncle, my pony's braided bridle, the gold cross I'd worn under my shirt since I was a baby. One night I saved my tapioca dessert and took it to her when she called for me. She ate it like a starving woman, gobbled it down. I had never seen her gobble anything. And then she vomited it all back at me.

"She had taken to her bed by then, Helena. When she called for me, I always thought she might be dead by the time I walked the long hall to her room. I understood she would die, even though I didn't understand what that meant.

"Sometimes, when a maid took me away from my play or dinner, or called to me when I was riding my pony, I wished my mother dead. I didn't want to sit by her bed anymore in the dark room. The smell was awful. I hated her for being sick and I was filled with guilt for wishing her dead. I prayed every night for forgiveness, but I knew God wouldn't give it to me. I was a wicked boy for wishing my mother dead.

"I'd have cut off a finger if she'd asked. But I still wished her dead."

Helena could see the child Roberto, the boy alone with his dying mother, his father absent. She saw Roberto as the little child he was, offering the treasures of his small life to his desperate mother. Helena's heart, so silent to every-thing but her own pain, shuddered in the hollow of her chest, as if beating for the first time.

And she began to weep for her husband.

✦ ✦ ✦

That night, Helena dreamed of Luis. Slumped at the foot of her tower stairs, she did not moan or stir, but lay in a sleep deeper than any she had known since she was a child. She moved only once, when a strong wind rushed down the stairs, lifting her damp hair off her quiet face. She turned her head to face the wind, nothing more.

Up in her tower room, the great angel's wings swept across the dusty floor, then into the high reaches of the tower's ceiling. The tower trembled, threatening to collapse under the powerful thrust of wings. Through the rest of the house, a low hum reverberated, the sound of an angel voice released at last, singing to his lady.

Roberto felt the thrumming within his house, as if the walls themselves were singing a song of the earth, a song as deep as the clay taken to form Gabriel. The house, so silent after Luis' death, had found its voice again. And Helena dreamed her dream of Luis.

Luis came to her exactly as he looked the last day she saw him—not smaller, not younger or older. The same child he was the last night she kissed him in his bed and sent him, unaware, to his death.

She dreamed him, but he was not a dream. He stood before her, her living child. She smelled the perfume of his skin after his evening bath, felt the round muscles of his arms and legs, heard his laughter and shouts as he gazed up at her. He smiled and she saw that he was happy.

She knew she could touch him, but she did not. She didn't need to. Their hands met without touching. She drew him to her while still seeing him from a distance. She bent to kiss his eyelids, mouth, the top of his head, his fingers, while he watched from afar with shining eyes. Her arms circled him as though to comfort him, and she felt herself comforted, rocked, soothed and lulled. She fell back into deep sleep with his fragrance surrounding her.

When she awoke in the morning, she knew what she must do.

Chapter 29

✦ ✦ ✦

Down in her kitchen, the cook was searching the drawer of her battered table. Her best shears, the ones strong enough to snap small bones, were not in their usual place. She looked through the drawer once more, with its familiar collection of worn wooden spoons, graters for nutmeg and cinnamon, sharp knives. The shears were not there.

✦ ✦ ✦

Up in the tower, Helena drew the heavy shears from under her nightgown. She was standing in front of Gabriel, looking at him, not at the instrument clutched in her hand. She stared directly into his eyes, did not blink though he gazed at her without compassion.

She laid the shears at the back of her neck, bent her head forward as if in supplication, pulled her long braid taut and began cutting through the thick hair. Her movements were deliberate.

"Never cut your hair," she heard her mother say. "It is your crown, your shining glory from God, Helena. Do not wear it loose. Bind it up always. You must not wear it in pride."

Her mother had brushed Helena's hair over and over with her own silver brush, trimmed the ends with tiny gold scissors. "Loosen it only for your husband. It will entangle him so he cannot leave you."

Helena did not breathe. Her tower stood still, did not follow the sun's wheeling arc. A long time passed with no sound but the measured rasp of metal to metal, the silver blades slicing through the sheaf of hair like a scythe swinging through tall grass.

Helena's braid swung free in her left hand. She looked up at her angel, then fell to her knees. She bent over her braid as though protecting it. It lay heavy in her hands, dead. Helena's head felt so light she was almost dizzy, unmoored. She raised her eyes to Gabriel's face. She lifted her hands, held up her shorn hair like a child sacrificed. A wail escaped her throat, rose higher. She swayed on her knees, sank to the hard plank floor.

She did not know how long she lay there, knew only that she had been there and then was not. She felt herself lifted up, not harshly but firmly, and set down on sore hands and scraped knees. She began to crawl away from Gabriel.

When she reached the small bed, with its dented pillow, its rumpled white coverlet, she did not lift herself into it. She lowered herself flat onto the floor, lay with cheek resting on the dusty wood, slid one hand and arm under the bed.

The box was still there, exactly where she had hidden it. Helena opened the lid and inhaled the perfumes of her sin—linseed oil, turpentine, fresh pigments encased in smooth silver tubes. High cerulean blue, lush alizarin crimson, fresh greens and tangy yellows, pale violet, tender rose. The rich and tempting paint box of Tomás.

She ran bruised fingers over the tubes, the crumpled, pungent cleaning rags, the wooden paint palette with its stain of colors from her last work, the portrait of Célia. Her hands hovered over the rows of paints, each with its promise of delicious release into a forbidden world. She chose none of them, stopped instead at Tomás' brushes.

She lifted out the smallest brush, a slender reed with a few thin strands in its metal band. The wooden handle, slim though it was, held a memory in its grain of her hand and Tomás' hand. The two of them sharing brushes and pigment, bread and air.

She dropped the brush as though burned by its touch. Took in one deep breath and grabbed it again roughly. She picked up the kitchen shears and cut the bristles from the brush. She reached for her braid, unwound a clump of hair from the end, snipped it carefully with the large shears and began binding them to the slender handle with waxed thread.

By the time the cook found her—running up the tower steps with Carmelinha close behind —Helena had made twelve brushes with her own hair. Each one had cost her. There were red marks across her palms as though a brand had been laid on them.

The two women cried out when they saw her, saw the blunt, hacked ends of hair where her braid had been.

The cook rushed to take the shears from her, but Helena stopped her with a stare.

"Your beautiful hair," Carmelinha said.

"Never mind that," Helena said, looking not at her but at the cook. "Bring me my easel and canvases."

Chapter 30

+ + +

Helena attacked the painting in a white heat. She hastily sketched in three figures, threw down the charcoal, tore lids off paint tubes.

Throughout the house, the maids could hear her panting as she mixed smoldering colors on her slivered palette. She groped for a clean brush, filled it with paint, laid the first wet stroke of color on the canvas. She inhaled deeply, laid on a second lashing of paint. Knew, suddenly and without question, that she would see this through.

She began with her son. Carmelinha had brought her the photographs of Luis with Roberto and José, but Helena did not need them. Luis stood brightly before her canvas, a vision to be graced with color. Luis, precious Luis, waiting for Helena to breath life into him with her paints.

Her hand moved from palette to canvas, palette to canvas, developing a steady rhythm. Her breathing slowed. She had no question of colors to use, no hesitation over the brushes. She was the runner heading into the long climb, the angel beating his wings ceaselessly against the wind.

Her head throbbed. Heat moved through her body, fueled her, guided her swollen hand as it dipped into Tomás' paints. The voice of Tomás was with her.

"Remember the bones, Helena. Leonardo painted from the bones out."

She first tried to ignore the voice, paint through it. She finally began to listen to it, sensing it was coming not from her teacher but from the same source that guided her hand.

"Look to the anatomy, Helena. See your boy as bones and cartilage, muscle and tendons."

She submitted to the instruction. Her hand heard the voice. Her heart was quiet as she painted the bones of Luis, bones she had first felt forming in her own belly before anyone else suspected she was carrying a child. She painted his small muscles, his soft skin and hair. She caressed his face with the brushes of her own hair, tenderly pressed them against his eyelids, his cheeks, his mouth, then his neck and solid torso, the round arms and legs just emerging from baby fat into the young man he would never become.

Carmelinha brought her a tray with black bean soup and hot bread, the same food she would give to Roberto when he arrived home. He and his wife would both let their meals go cold, uneaten. Helena heard Roberto come to take up his vigil and Carmelinha tell him the story of the day. Heard him push against the door, which was still locked to him.

She did not go down her steps to the door. She stayed at her easel, seeing her husband not as the man huddled beyond the door, but as a figure barely sketched onto a canvas. A figure there only to fill in the air beside Luis.

She worked into the night, with no mind to rest.

While darkness hung outside her tower, she painted Luis bathed in a clear light, a light she now understood had always shone on him. He had been marked from the beginning as a Leonardo angel. The sign of ownership was as sure as the small birthmark he and José shared. A boy to be treasured and a boy to be taken. She had been spared the sight and knowledge of the light while her child lived. To recognize it would have driven her mad.

When Luis stood alive before her at last, when he radiated from the canvas with fresh skin and clear eyes, Helena turned to Roberto and José. She started, almost carelessly, to create the shapes around her luminous son, Roberto seated beside him in the armchair, José beyond Roberto and slightly apart.

In the hours before dawn, the two figures took on weight. Roberto, seated in his heavy chair, looked as solid as the chair, a man of bone and muscle. José was a young animal, ready to leap off the canvas in delight or fear. Both became human, tissue and blood.

As Roberto and José began breathing on the canvas, Luis was transfigured. Helena saw color fade from his eyes, his rosy lips, his face and body. She did not stop to grieve the fresh loss. She continued to paint through the pain in her hand, as sunlight filtered through her high window, creeping into the dusty corners of her tower room.

She painted until there was nothing left to paint, until the voice guiding her hand was silent. And then she stepped back and saw what she was meant to see.

One boy, so ephemeral as to be nothing but light, translucent and holy. Beside him, two people—one grown, one small—with the same face, the same mouth, same strong jaw and chin, same long fine nose. Above all, the same dark eyes, looking out at her from two faces formed of the same clay, the same bone and blood.

Helena dropped her brush, put her face in her tired hands, stood quiet and trembling until she could compose herself. Then she turned her easel to face her bed and sat down on the rumpled spread.

Slowly and without thought, she opened herself to the painting, let it enter her skin, seep into her blood stream. She inhaled it, as if she were sitting down to a meal of many courses. Tasted its complicated flavors, the sweet and the bitter.

A father, staring out from the canvas in pride and a barely controlled anger, as though he could see what would befall the careful kingdom he had constructed for himself and his family.

Her husband, handsome and good. A man who had taken her in hope and love, who had tried to make a perfect world for her and failed, as she had failed him.

On one side of him, an incandescent child, a boy so pure the world would ache to lose him. On the other side, a child with his father's face, eyes filled with hope, courage and bewilderment.

Helena sat until the day was full upon the world outside her tower and the light full upon her canvas. And then she rose from her bed, walked slowly down her stairs, and opened the door to her sleeping husband.

Roberto stumbled awake, stood up abruptly. Stared down at her, unable to speak. She took his hand and led him up the staircase. They faced the painting together, with one set of eyes, looking at a family in a ruined house.

After a time, Roberto turned away from the painting and gazed down at the ravaged woman standing with him.

"Helena," he said. The word died in his throat. He said nothing for a moment, then began again. "I shouldn't have let you bring José into this house. Perhaps it put a blight on our lives, this child I may have…"

Helena reached up, pressed her bruised fingers against his lips.

"Hush, now," she said, as if talking to her child.

He took her hand in his, looked at the torn nails, the scorched palm.

"Your hand," he said, brokenly.

"We were foolish, Roberto. We betrayed what we had. Now we will ask for forgiveness and pray that we may be redeemed. We will do what we must."

She turned back to the painting, the last she would ever create. She looked at the family in the painting, and then she looked at her husband, standing gray and somber beside her.

"Please bring José home," she said. "Bring him home to us where he belongs."

ACKNOWLEDGEMENTS

✦ ✦ ✦

My grateful thanks to all who stood by me through the years that *Angel* was coming to life.

To my three compassionate friends who nudged both me and my book into the world - Josephine Jones, Norma Douglas and Carole Skinner. To my three supportive "after-school" teachers - Jonis Agee, Joan Logghe and Cathy Wagner. To my three discerning editors - Jeanette Germain, Peter Guzzardi and Adrienne Brodeur. And to my three wise women - Nancy Stringfellow, Jean Wilson and Jane Oppenheimer.

To my long-time writing buddy and champion, Alan Minskoff, and the rest of the writing group who gathered around Ruth Wright's table - Chris Dempsey, Barbara Herrick, Gino Sky, Colleen Birch Maile and Steven Mayfield.

To my circle of friends who listened with good cheer and advice as I continued the book journey - Carolyn Cannon and Pug Ostling, Royanne Minskoff, Leah Clark and her sweet family, Edith Hope, Elizabeth Clarke, Chris Binion, Gay Rigby Whitesides, Alvin Greenberg and Janet Holmes, Nancy Van Dinter, Jan English, Chris Latter, Judy Wold, Clay Morgan, John Rember, Diane Josephy Peavey, Nancy Oakes, Regina Brown, Grove Koger and astronomer Jeff Craig.

And to my wonderful publisher Elaine Ambrose - a joy to work with and a joy to know - and her talented designer, Sarah Tregay, and editor, Amanda Turner.